THE FARMER'S BRIDE
The Flat River Matchmaker #1

Christine Sterling

THE FARMER'S BRIDE
© 2022 CHRISTINE STERLING

Cover Design by Virginia McKevitt,
Editing by Carolyn Leggo, Amy Petrowich, and Amber Downey
1st Ed. 7/2022

www.flatrivernebraska.com

TABLE OF CONTENTS

GET FREE BOOKS

Do you love wholesome romance, funny stories, and want a new recipe each week? Join Christine's newsletter and get a free copy of <u>Not His Mail Order Bride</u>, from the *First Families of Flat River* series. https://dl.bookfunnel.com/gsk52ipap6

The Farmer's Bride

A woman needing a home; a man needing a helpmate and a marriage of convenience that meets both of their needs.

Forced from her home, Elizabet Garrett needs to find a husband, and fast. What she doesn't anticipate is meeting a man who is nothing like she expects, but just might be the answer to her prayers.

Disabled after a farming accident, Peter Arkin lives on his small homestead nursing his demons and a broken dream. Forced to face another harsh winter alone, he sobers up and agrees to allow a local matchmaker to find a suitable mail-order bride. But hurtful rejections for his handicap leaves him reluctant to keep trying.

Does he have enough faith to take one more chance? Will Elizabet be able to see beyond his injury and be the helpmate he needs? Is there a chance that they can find the love and healing they both desperately seek? Find out in this small-town historical romance with a touch of faith.

CHAPTER ONE

July 1875, Flat River, Nebraska

"She can't stay here."

Elizabet Garrett gasped as Lucinda's words filled the small room. She had just returned from collecting berries by the creek when the horrible words carried to the dimly lit area by the back door of the three-room house.

She pressed her back to the wall and strained her ears to hear the conversation occurring in hushed tones. She heard her brother's boots thud across the floor, blocking Elizabet's view of her very pregnant sister-in-law. The door was slightly open, and she scurried to the other side, lest she be seen eavesdropping.

She had been living with her brother since she was

thirteen in the tiny home along the edge of the woods. The following year he married Lucinda Jones and there were three of them cramped in the tiny house. She couldn't believe it had been nearly five years.

It wasn't her fault that their parents died, and she had to travel across the country to the only family she had left. *Now it appeared, they didn't want her.*

Her brother, Todd, was eight years her senior. He left Virginia right after the war between the states to settle in the Nebraska Territory. When he heard about their parents passing, he didn't hesitate to send for Elizabet and bring her to live with him. Unfortunately, it was something he didn't mention to his fiancée, Lucinda.

Elizabet knew that Lucinda wasn't happy sharing a house, or Todd's attention, with anyone else. Even if that anyone else was a thirteen-year-old girl with nowhere to go. When Todd finally married Lucinda, a few weeks later, it became very crowded in the small saltbox house.

"Lucinda," Todd Garrett warned. "We've been through this before. Elizabet's my sister. Where else would she go?"

"I don't know. Can't she go back to Virginia? We are going to have a baby." Elizabet tried not to roll her eyes at the nasally sound of her sister-in-law's whining. "We need the extra room."

"There is no home to go to. Everything was sold. She had no family, very few friends. That is why she came out here." She heard her brother sigh. "We said we were going to wait to have a family until Elizabet was older."

"She's nearly eighteen! Why, I was married to you when I turned seventeen. If she stays any longer, she's going to be a spinster." Lucinda threw her hands in the air. "What then? No one will have her, and you'll be responsible for her the rest of her days. She's not pretty enough to catch a husband on her own."

"Lucinda, that's enough. I will not have any more talk like that. She's my sister and I'm not going to send her away."

"She can go work at Miss Marcy's. I hear she is always looking for new help."

Elizabet heard Todd growl from behind the door. She cowed as his heavy boots thudded across the floor, and she wasn't even in the room. "You get that foolish notion out of your head. My sister will never work there." His voice sounded menacing.

"Todd, I do love Elizabet, but it is just too much having an extra person in our house. I thought she would have either gotten married or moved somewhere else by now."

"We will figure something out. Let me talk to Elizabet first."

Elizabet could hear the exhaustion in Lucinda's voice. "I'm going to lay down, Todd. I'm very tired."

"Do I need to fetch the doctor?" Concern was evident in Todd's voice. Elizabet peeked her head through the doorframe to see Lucinda shake her head, dark curls bouncing around her ears.

"I just need to rest. Perhaps you can talk to her on your own and decide on what's going to happen. I just know it is time for you to focus on your own family. We will need the room when the baby arrives."

Elizabet waited until she heard the door close to the bedroom before coming out of the shadows and walking into the kitchen. She put the basket on the table and made a show of removing her bonnet and shawl.

Todd looked at her with sad eyes. "How much of that did you hear?"

"Enough," she said, hanging her hat and shawl by the door.

"I think she's getting melancholy as the birth approaches. It doesn't have anything to do with you."

Elizabet fidgeted, her fingers worrying her skirt fabric. "But it does. I understand she wants a house of her own. It is only natural for a married woman. What she said is true. You need the extra room for the nursery…"

"Elizabet, please," her brother began.

Elizabet raised her hand. "Let me finish. A woman needs her own space, not one where she is being crowded by other people."

Todd quirked his lips in a half-smile. "Are you talking about Lucy, or you?"

"Maybe both." Elizabet fetched a mug and filled it with coffee before sitting down at the table. She looked at her brother. "After Pa died, I didn't know where I was going to go. I was destined for the poor house after paying his debts. The only thing I had left was the townhouse, and even the bank took that. I was sure I was going to be sent to the factories." Todd joined her at the small table. "I am so grateful that you allowed me to come here and live with you. But Lucinda is right, I need to find my own place."

"I don't want you to think we are pushing you out," Todd said softly. "What are you thinking? There isn't much around here."

Elizabet shrugged her shoulders. That was true. Flat River was a very small town, consisting of a few ranches, several businesses in town and a large saloon with a bordello upstairs. Most of the men were hard working cowboys. The businessmen in town were much older and already married. Elizabet winced. Working at Miss Marcy's would be her last resort.

"I don't know. Maybe I'll find a cowboy to marry." Todd raised his eyebrow and looked at her. A cowboy himself, he made sure that Elizabet didn't spend much time around cowboys when she arrived at Flat River. She lowered her chin and looked at her brother through thick lashes. "Perhaps I should be a mail-order bride. It worked for you."

"A what?" Todd's voice rose.

"Shhh," Elizabet admonished. "Lucy is resting." She took a sip of her coffee before placing the mug on the table. "It is not uncommon for a woman to answer an advertisement for a man seeking a wife. Did you know that there are even entire papers devoted to just such a thing?"

"But a stranger, Elizabet?" Todd dragged his hand down his face. He was a very handsome man, looking just like their father. Elizabet took after her mother with her reddish-blonde hair and green eyes. "I don't like the idea of you moving somewhere to marry a stranger."

"Then what do you suggest?"

"I don't know. Maybe we could speak to Marmee?"

"Marmee? That's a splendid idea."

Weston Chapman owned one of the largest ranches in Flat River. His wife, Ingrid, insisted that everyone call her *Marmee,* and she was viewed as surrogate mother to many of the men that worked her ranch.

"Marmee knows all about these things. She will know what to do."

"What are you suggesting? That she finds me a husband?"

"It might be worth paying a visit to her. You might want to make a list of what you are looking for in someone. She might be able to find the right person."

"Do you think she can find someone here in town?"

"I don't know. But she can help write an advertisement."

"What's wrong with a cowboy, Todd? You're a cowboy."

Todd pulled his hand down his face. "You want a strong man, with good values, Lizzy. I've been around these cowboys for a long time. If there is a cowboy that has what you need, Marmee will know someone."

"I'm sure an advertisement costs money."

"Let's talk to her first. I have a few coins put aside if you need them. We can go see her in the morning."

Elizabet finished her coffee. "I'll get everything cleaned up. You go check on Lucy."

Todd pushed the chair away from the table. "You know she loves you, don't you?" Elizabet nodded, too overcome with emotion to speak. He leaned down and pressed a kiss to the top of Elizabet's head. "I love you too, sweet sister."

Elizabet stared at her hands wrapped around the enamel mug as she listened to Todd's footsteps cross the hard floor and disappear into the room. Sighing, she stood and walked over to the dry sink. A large enamel tub sitting on top of a wooden cabinet, Todd had designed it, especially for Lucy. There wasn't a spigot, so water still needed to be drawn from outside and heated on the stove. The bottom of the bowl, however, had a drain that carried the dirty dishwater away.

Elizabet thought it was an ingenious setup, and preferred washing dishes in the large tub instead of two buckets, as she did when she was living in Virginia. She washed the dishes from dinner and then scrubbed the Dutch oven before putting it back on the stove to dry.

She recalled what Todd said. *Make a list of everything you would like in a husband.*

There were the standard attributes she was sure

any woman would want. Someone handsome and self-sufficient. He would be kind to both children and animals. He would be strong and a protector. She hoped he had a dry sink in his house. And enough room that if anyone needed to stay, they could stay for as long as they wanted, without causing a disturbance.

She would have to write these down in her journal, so she remembered them when they went to go see Marmee in the morning.

Grabbing the wet cloth, she wiped down the table and set the coffee pot up so all she had to do was add water in the morning. Looking around the room, she didn't see anything else she needed to do, so she blew out the lamp on the table and made her way through the darkness to her small room.

The glow from a lamp on the corner table filled the room. Her trunk sat at the foot of a small bed covered with a worn quilt. Looking at the flat mattress, Elizabet missed the bed she had growing up, with its down pillows and soft duvet. Now she was sleeping on straw wrapped in a ticked bedsheet.

Wrinkling her nose, she undressed and hung her clothes on a peg next to the door. There wasn't enough room for a wardrobe in the small room, so Elizabet kept her clothes in the trunk. Rummaging through the box, she pulled out her nightgown and lifted it above her head, shimmying it down to her ankles. After saying her prayers, she extinguished the light and crawled beneath the covers. Todd's words filled Elizabet's thoughts as she pulled a coarse blanket up to her chin.

Marmee will know what to do.

She just hoped that her brother was correct.

CHAPTER TWO

"I still cannot believe you did this, Marmee," Peter Arkin grumbled, shifting on the bench to get in a more comfortable spot. He glanced at his pocket watch. The stage from Grand Platte should be arriving shortly. It wouldn't be long before he'd see dust rising in the air. "You would think that there'd be a train coming to Flat River by now. We aren't living in the Middle Ages."

"Progress is slow, Mr. Arkin," Ingrid Chapman, known as Marmee by everyone in Flat River said, her silver curls bouncing beneath her bonnet.

"And it is passing right by this little Podunk town," he mumbled under his breath.

He shifted on the hard wooden bench once more. The stump that was once his leg hung limply over the side, and his crutches leaned against the wall of the mercantile. He winced, the phantom pain never quite going away. He should be used to it by now; after all, it had been just over a year since the accident that took his leg. He was running out of money and options.

He could still recall the moment he lost his footing and his leg caught underneath the sharp blade of the plow. His life changed forever in that instance. It didn't matter how many times he heard how fortunate he was – the plow completely severed the leg beneath the knee with surgical precision. It didn't matter how many times he heard stories of others whose legs were so mangled they gave up hope and died, Peter Arkin survived.

He didn't feel fortunate.

He recalled pressing his leg against the cold steel of the plow to stop the flow of blood until he passed out in the dirt. He didn't know how long he was in the field until he woke up in the back of a wagon with Doc cauterizing his leg. The scent of burning flesh still filled his nostrils and he knew it would never leave him.

But that fateful day, Peter lost more than his lower leg. He lost his confidence. His sense of purpose. *His faith.*

He refused to leave the house until he heard noise in the yard. Peeking outside the curtains, he couldn't believe what he was seeing. There must have been at least a dozen men in the field.

Peter hobbled out to the edge of the porch. The sight was almost too much to bear. It should be him in the field, not his neighbors.

Four men with large grain cradles moved slowly, swinging their blades back and forth. When the cradles were full, two men pulled up behind them and tied the straw into large bundles, before dropping the shocks onto the field to dry.

Weston Chapman had organized the neighbors to help harvest the wheat. With the number of men working, the entire ten acres was harvested before sundown. Women stopped by to feed the men and check on Peter.

They feasted on thick ham sandwiches, fresh apples from the trees that grew by the river, homemade cookies and mason jars filled with milk or sweet lemonade. Leftovers were wrapped up and left in Peter's kitchen, so he didn't have to worry about meals.

He hated accepting charity, but those were the kind of people that lived in Flat River. They looked out for each other. When the task was done, it was Weston Chapman that approached Peter about purchasing his entire wheat harvest. Weston even paid extra to allow his longhorn cattle to pasture on Peter's land and graze on the winter wheat during the colder months.

Peter was overwhelmed by the gesture because it meant he didn't have to find someone to take the wheat to market and sell it. The extra funds allowed him to focus on getting through winter. Weston returned in the spring, but Peter wasn't sure that he wanted to grow wheat again.

But Weston wasn't to be denied anything. He took one look at the empty bottles scattered around the small house and sent the one person who could get Peter back in shape to face the world.

Marmee.

No one ever went against Marmee.

No one.

She had him sober in two months and now there was a woman on her way to Flat River to marry him.

Peter leaned down and rubbed the stump of his leg, the coarse fabric scraping against his scar. Grimacing, he wondered if he would have been better wearing the wooden contraption Doc rigged up for him. As he rubbed, his fingertips brushed against the ridge where the wooden leg normally rested.

Doc suggested padding around the area with thick pieces of cotton fabric before putting on the leg, but all that did was provide something to wick perspiration down between the device and his flesh. During the sweltering summer heat, his leg would sweat against the wood, rubbing his skin raw with a pain so intense, Peter saw stars behind his eyelids as his fingers touched the sore skin.

Peter didn't want to risk infection setting in, so he preferred to use his crutches. *Besides*, it would be interesting to see his new bride's face when she got a look at what her future husband was really like.

A cripple.

"Excuse me?" Marmee said, interrupting his pity party. "Podunk town?"

"Sorry, Marmee," Peter said sheepishly. He felt Marmee's hand on his shoulder, patting it gently, and he glanced up at the older woman. She and her husband came to the area on a wagon train when the town had only a dozen people. They stayed, along with several other wagons, and the town doubled in size that very day. Since then, it had grown to nearly one hundred people. Peter was sure that nearly half of those were cowboys and the other half were employed by the brothel in town.

"I know it is hard, Peter." There was something about her voice that was soothing. It was almost like a lullaby. He closed his eyes and listened. "Flat River is small, but that's what makes it special. It's like one large family." She patted his shoulder. "And as a family, we look out for each other. You shouldn't be out at that farm all alone. It is good that you finally decided to send for a helpmate."

Helpmate. Help.

Helpless.

He snorted and pushed himself up against the wall as if the very act made him taller. Not one to ask for help, it appeared he had little choice now. He would need help to get through the winter. After the accident, the townspeople rallied around him for a bit, but they had their own houses and farms to manage. Winters could be harsh, and Peter was lonely. He wanted a wife and sons, but that was before. Now he didn't know what marriage would entail, as he was half the man he used to be.

Marmee suggested maybe he should find a helpmate. A woman to help on the farm, but women were scarce in Flat River, except at Miss Marcy's. He had no desire to find a woman from among the soiled doves. He knew several cowboys found women there, but he wanted a different type of woman.

An honorable woman.

A godly woman.

Marmee took it upon herself to find him someone,

and now that woman was on her way to Flat River to marry him. He read most of the correspondence, but Marmee made the match.

"How will I know her again?" he asked.

"She said she would wear a yellow dress."

"Yellow." Peter rolled the word around on his tongue. "And her name was Madeline?" Marmee nodded. It seemed like such a formal name. *Madeline in a yellow dress.* He turned his attention back towards the road to see if he could see the approaching stagecoach, his fingers continuing in a circular pattern along his stump. "Might be better off alone," he mumbled under his breath.

"Nonsense, Peter," Marmee said, patting his arm. "The good Lord didn't mean for a man to be alone. That's why he created a helpmate for Adam."

His eyes scanned the horizon, squinting as he willed something… anything, to appear. Finally, he could see a cloud of dust in the distance, from where the hooves kicked up the dirt along the trail.

"I think that might be them!" He could feel the tension filling his chest. He turned to Marmee, who was waving to a young woman walking towards the store. Peter recalled seeing her around town once or twice but didn't know the young woman's name.

She jumped on the platform and stood next to

Marmee. "Good afternoon, Marmee," she said, nodding to Peter in greeting as well. "It is a lovely afternoon."

"It is, Elizabet," Marmee agreed. "How's your sister-in-law?"

Peter couldn't help but notice the sadness that appeared over the young woman's features. She was rather young, couldn't be a minute over sixteen. Her face was scrubbed clean, and Peter noticed she had freckles dotting her nose. Wisps of yellow hair escaped her chignon, and she brushed them away with a gloved hand, but he noticed the tear she wiped away as well. The thought of something hurting this young lady pained him, although he couldn't explain why. He had no business with her.

"She's just exhausted. I know she'll be glad when the baby arrives."

"Babies are blessings, indeed."

"Indeed," the woman called Elizabet said softly. "Marmee, my brother suggested I talk to you. I was wondering if I might take a bit of your time?"

The sound of thunder filled the air. From the corner of his eye, Peter saw the cloud of dust rise from the dry ground as the coach approached the town, but his ear still picked up bits of the surrounding conversation.

"Of course, child," Marmee said. "I have a bit of

business to attend to, and then how about you come back to the house with me, and we'll have a spot of tea?"

The rest of the words drowned under horses' hooves and wooden wheels as the driver pulled alongside the mercantile. Another man rode next to him, cradling a two-barrel shotgun in one arm as he held onto the side of the bench with his hand.

"Whoa!" The driver pulled on the reins, slowing the stagecoach in front of the mercantile. He set the brake and then turned to face the storefront. "Hiya, Rose!" he called, grabbing a box from the seat next to him before leaning over the side of the wooden bench. "I have a box for you. Came from New York City."

Peter turned to see Rose Arden, who ran the mercantile with her husband, Dillon, move past him. "Must be my fabric samples," she said, taking the box and stuffing it under one arm. "Came from France. I'm hoping to expand the fabrics we offer soon."

The driver snorted as he shifted in the seat. "I don't think there are enough women in town to warrant bolts of cloth from France." He leaned over the back of his seat and grabbed a rucksack, tossing it to the ground. "Not a lot of mail this time."

"Did my medicine arrive from Denver?" Doc asked, coming around the back of the stage.

"It did." The driver handed Doc a box and he looked at it before walking back to his office.

Rose handed the driver a stack of letters. "That's all we have for today. Do you have time for a cup of coffee?"

The driver shook his head. "Not this time. I gotta make Maxwell in two days. Looks like I'll be driving all night."

"At least refill your coffee and I'll put sandwiches in a napkin for you. What about you?" She pointed her box at the man on the bench.

"Just coffee, ma'am," he said, tipping his hat.

The driver handed Rose two quart jars with coffee stains coating the inside. "Appreciate that, Rose."

Peter shifted in the seat. He knew this was the same routine, but his impatience was getting the best of him. "You got any passengers with you today?" Peter growled.

The driver jumped from the seat to the ground, landing with a thud. "Just one. Let me get her out and then I'll be on my way."

Peter held his breath as the driver dropped a step under the door and opened the latch. A large group of yellow feathers appeared in the door.

Was it a bird?

The feathers bobbed from side to side, and the form of a woman appeared from the dark interior.

A gloved hand lifted a yellow skirt trimmed in lace and Peter spied a slender ankle encased in leather reach down to the step. She handed her bag to the driver and held onto the door as she stepped to the hard ground. She lifted her head, and the feathers swayed from side to side.

That was the most ridiculous thing Peter had ever seen.

There were enough feathers on her hat to dust the entire mercantile! She reminded Peter of a canary his mother kept in a cage near the window. Her movements were quick as a bird too as she moved to the back of the stagecoach, close to the platform, where Peter was sitting.

He glanced up at Marmee who smiled at him, giving him an encouraging nod. The woman wrinkled her nose as she looked around the town. "It's much smaller than I imagined," she said, snapping open a parasol and lifting it over the feathers. "And dusty. I can't believe the dust on the trip." She shook out her skirt with her free hand. "I'll be tasting dust for days. How can anyone live in a town so small?"

"It's just big enough for the people that live here," Marmee responded. "We have everything a small town needs. A store, a doctor, a church. Welcome to Flat River. You must be Madeline." The woman spied Marmee and moved forward. The feathers bounced out of the way and Peter could see the woman had dark hair peeking out from underneath the outlandish bonnet. She was pretty enough, with large dark eyes, a pert nose, and lips that were pressed in a thin line. Peter couldn't even see the color of her lips her mouth was so tight.

"I was supposed to meet my intended here," she said, exhaling loudly. She looked around at the men moving away from the platform. "Is he here?" She looked at Marmee hopefully. "I am looking forward to taking a bath."

Peter took a deep breath and reached for his crutches, putting them in front of him. With a grunt, he lifted himself and slid the wooden supports under his arm. He should have used the silly wooden leg and dealt with the friction sores. Holding the crutches in place, he moved his good leg forward, then swung the crutches towards the porch edge. It took three steps before he was standing at the edge of the platform. He braced himself against the corner post and cleared his throat.

"Miss Cooper?" The woman turned, the feathers bobbing in unison under the parasol. Her gaze flickered to his missing leg and back to his face. Her shoulders tightened, and she raised her chin, looking down her nose at him. Her lips moved, but no sound came out. Peter called her name once more.

The woman's eyes snapped to his before glancing at Marmee as if looking for confirmation. Finally, she turned back to him. "Are you Mr. Arkin?"

Peter leaned against the post and scratched his chin, the whiskers tickling his fingers. *Perhaps he should have shaved?* Nodding, he smiled at her. "Yes, ma'am."

Madeline Cooper looked as though she might retch. She placed the back of her fist against her mouth and puffed out her cheeks. After several deep breaths, she lowered her hand and curled her lip. "You can't be Mr. Arkin," she snarled. "Why... why... look at you. You are crippled."

Peter stumbled back as if she had physically assaulted him. He heard a gasp from behind him and he glanced around the platform, embarrassment coloring his cheeks. The young woman was standing near the door. Her lips pursed in anger, but her eyes held pity as she watched him try to right himself with the crutches. He didn't have time to deal with her disgust as well.

He curled his shoulders as if protecting himself

from the verbal blows he knew were coming and turned back to Miss Cooper. "Yes ma'am. I am."

She shook her head, sending several feathers floating to the ground. "There is no way I am going to marry a cripple." The venom of her words slapped him across the face. "You should have said that in your letter. I would have never wasted my time in coming."

"Miss Cooper," Marmee said. "I mentioned it…"

"Marmee," Peter warned. "Leave it." It wasn't the first time someone had talked about him, and he was sure it wouldn't be the last. The words stung, but this time the words didn't bother him as much as they should have. He was better off knowing her true feelings before marrying her.

Shrugging his shoulders, he righted himself on his crutches. "I'm sorry you wasted your time, Miss Cooper."

The woman hurried to the door of the stagecoach. "Don't bother removing my trunk," she told the driver. "I'll be going to the next town." Peter watched her scramble back into the coach, slamming the door behind her. She glared at the small party standing on the platform and snapped the window shade down.

Peter dropped his chin. *Why did he let Marmee talk him into this again?* He lifted his shoulders, and he shook his head, willing the burning at the back of his throat to go away. "Thank you for trying, Marmee," he mumbled. "I know you did your best. I should get home."

What had he been hoping for? His eyes darted to the stump of what had once been his leg. *No one would want a cripple,* just as she had said. He turned on his crutch and hobbled towards the far side of the platform where his wagon waited.

"Peter, don't give up," Marmee pleaded. "I know…"

"Excuse me," the young woman he spied earlier moved towards them. "Did that woman come here to marry you?"

Peter paused. He stared at the younger woman, who was eyeing him intently. She wasn't as young as Peter first thought. Her hair, which he thought was yellow, was the color of wheat fields with a hint of cinnamon. Large green eyes peeked from behind dark lashes, with rosy circles dotting her cheeks. She reminded him of a porcelain doll.

"Didn't your parents teach you any manners?" he snapped.

"My parents are dead. I live with my brother and his wife."

Peter felt instantly ashamed. There was no reason for him to be rude to this young woman just because someone was rude to him. "My apologies, Miss," he said. It appeared today was filled with apologies.

"She will not marry you?"

Marmee quickly moved forward. "It's alright, Elizabet. It just means she wasn't the right one." She waved her hand in the air as if dismissing the notion.

"Peter, why don't you stop by the house and at least have dinner before you head home? I know Weston would love an opportunity to visit with you."

The young woman named Elizabet snaked her fingers around Marmee's arm. "Marmee, I was hoping you might help me with something," she said, her eyes glancing once more at Peter.

"I don't think now is a good time," Marmee said. "Why don't you stop by this week, and we can talk about whatever you need."

Peter saw her fingers tighten around Marmee's hand as she stared directly at him. His mouth opened as the last words he expected to hear from the young lady burst forth from her lips.

"I need a husband."

CHAPTER THREE

Elizabet took one last look around the room before closing her small bag. She didn't have much to pack, just a spare day dress and her boots and a few personal items. Everything else Lucinda insisted she leave. After all, the dresses were hand-me-downs and she would need them once the baby was born, more than Elizabet would on some dusty farm.

At least that is what Lucinda said.

Todd and Lucinda refused to be a part of the wedding. When Elizabet returned home after speaking with Marmee they were cautiously happy. When she mentioned that Marmee knew someone that needed a wife, they were pleased. As soon as Elizabet mentioned her future husband's name and that they were to be married the following day, she thought

Todd was going to grab his shotgun and go out to the Chapman ranch and confront Marmee.

Lucinda managed to calm him down, but she spent the rest of the evening in her room softly sobbing. Until it came time for Elizabet to pack. Then Lucinda scrutinized every item in the room that might leave *her* house.

Elizabet didn't understand. *Didn't she do what they wanted?* It wasn't worth fighting over. She vowed never to have a marriage built on conflict. It wasn't worth it. Both Todd and Lucinda just seemed miserable all the time.

Releasing a low sigh, she picked up her bag and walked out to the kitchen.

"I can't believe you are leaving." Todd sat at the kitchen table sulking with his hands wrapped around the coffee mug. He wouldn't lift his eyes to meet hers. "And to marry Peter Arkin?"

Elizabet dropped her bag next to the door and moved towards the table. "Where's Lucy?"

Todd didn't move his head. "She went to lie down."

"Of course, she did." She was tired of dealing with Lucinda's theatrics and now there was no reason to take part in them anymore.

"What do you mean by that? She's unwell." He shot her a venomous look.

Elizabet glanced to the door leading into her brother's room, noting it was opened slightly. Normally Lucinda kept it closed to minimize her contact with Elizabet, but her sister-in-law must want to hear what was being said.

"If she's so unwell, you would think she'd want someone to help her." She walked across the room and closed the door, pulling a little harder than necessary. "She's made it clear that she couldn't wait to get me out of the house. I'm surprised she isn't out here gloating."

"Eliza-"

"All I've heard for the past five years is *when am I going to leave*. I was thirteen years old. Thirteen, Todd." She pounded her fist on the table. "You were my only family. I had just arrived, and she wanted to know when I was going to leave. She was looking to get rid of me from the moment she set eyes on me. I never stopped you from marrying her. I never said anything unkind about her. Not once."

"Lizzy. You have to understand…"

"I don't have to understand a thing." She moved closer to the door and peered outside. "Mr. Arkin will be here soon."

"Mr. Arkin." Todd spat the name out like it was poison on his tongue. "Whatever made you choose him I don't know. Most women have their choice of who they could marry. Look at Lucy. She could have married anyone. I had obligations, but she waited. I was…" He swallowed, a large lump bobbing in his throat.

"Fortunate?" she supplied, raising her eyebrow. "Well, I hope she can manage it."

"What do you mean?"

"She'll have a baby to tend to, while taking care of everything in the house. The only time she ever worked was when you were home."

"Lucinda will do just fine, I'm sure." Elizabet snorted at that remark, as her brother glared at her even harder. "At least she won't be taking care of a cripple. How is this broken farmer even going to support you?"

"Mr. Arkin is an honorable man."

"How will he be able to take care of you?"

Elizabet shrugged. "I assume as any other man would."

"How will he make a living with only one leg? What about children? Can he even give you any?"

"Todd!" Elizabet thinned her lips so hard they hurt. Where was her gentle brother? He would never look down on anyone before. Elizabet didn't say anything else. She wanted to defend the man who was to be her husband, but she knew no matter what she said, Todd would find something to counter it. Better to let it just go.

"I'll do just fine, Mr. Garrett." His strong voice filled the small room.

Elizabet whirled around so quickly her legs caught in the fabric of her skirt. She stumbled and caught herself on one of the chairs next to the table. Her fingers curled around the top rail as she saw Peter Arkin filling the entire doorframe.

Oh, land! He was taller than she imagined. His head brushed the top of the door, which Elizabet knew to be six feet, three inches to accommodate the father that lived there before Todd purchased the house. She couldn't see Mr. Arkin's features as the sun cast a shadow across his frame, but she could see that his jaw was firmly set as he reached a hand up to scratch at his cheek. Suddenly it dawned on her.

How long had he been standing there? How much had he overheard? Shame flooded her cheeks. What he must think about her family. Before she could say anything, Todd quickly pushed back from the table, knocking his coffee cup over. Elizabet instinctively reached for a rag to wipe up the hot liquid but stopped herself.

Why should she? It wasn't her home anymore.

"Arkin," Todd said.

"You're here." Her voice came out as a breathy whisper. She didn't have a doubt he would come, but to see him there made all her fears dissipate. *She was going to have her own home.*

"I told you I would be." His voice washed over her like warm honey in summer. He moved back into the sunlight just outside the door. "Is this your bag?" he asked, pointing to the carpetbag on the floor. Elizabet nodded. He picked it up and turned on his heel. "Grab your wrap and let's go."

Elizabet took her wrap from a peg and placed it over her arm. She stepped outside into the sunshine with Todd close on her heels. It was early enough in the day that the hot air hadn't given to the humidity Nebraska was known for.

Mr. Arkin paused and put the bag in the back of the buckboard. He rummaged in the back for a moment and turned, smiling at Elizabet with a smile that turned her insides to jelly. In his hand he held a bouquet of wild daisies, the stems still wet. He held them out towards her, water droplets rolling across his fingers.

"I thought every bride should have a bouquet."

Elizabet blushed. "Thank you." No one had ever given her flowers. She couldn't even recall Todd ever bringing flowers to Lucinda. She brought the bouquet up to her face and inhaled deeply, the pollen tickling her nose. "They are beautiful."

She looked back at the man she was going to marry. She thought he was very handsome in a dark suit with his hair combed back. He had rich brown hair with the same color eyes. His skin was pale, probably because he hadn't been outside much since losing his leg. But he was handsome. *Oh, so handsome!*

"Let me help you in the wagon," he offered gently, holding his hand out.

As she moved closer, she noticed a large wooden foot protruded from beneath his dark trousers. Her eyes flew up to meet his. "Where are your crutches?" she asked, realizing he wasn't using them.

"I thought today was important enough that I needed to wear this," he tapped his wooden foot on the ground.

"Why didn't you wear it yesterday?" she whispered.

He smiled at her, revealing strong white teeth. "Sometimes it hurts. My leg was sore yesterday."

Elizabet moved closer to the wagon, careful to avoid stepping on the wooden appendage. "Does it hurt today?"

"Like the dickens. But it's not every day a man gets married." He reached over and took her hand to assist her into the wagon. Warmth enveloped her digits and spread up her arm like fireflies. Elizabet tried to move, but her feet wouldn't budge.

"Just see here," Todd said, pushing Elizabet aside.

The warmth was gone in an instant, and she stumbled to the ground, her flowers scattering around her. "Oh!" she cried as her hand scraped on the hard dirt. "My flowers." She brushed the small rocks from her hand, her fingers tracing the grooves they left in her palm.

"Elizabet, I'm sorry," Todd said, kneeling beside her, crushing several of the flowers as he reached to help her up. Elizabet moved out of reach, wincing at the tenderness in her hand.

"I can get myself up, thank you," she scoffed. She scooted away, muttering under her breath at the dirt gathering on her clean dress. Mr. Arkin did not deserve a bride in a soiled wedding gown. The sky went dark, and she looked up to see a shadow looming over her.

"Let me help you." His voice was soft, but she could hear the undercurrent of anger in his tone.

She reached her hand up and the warmth returned. Mr. Arkin stepped back, and she found herself flying into his embrace. His leg stiffened to hold her as she pressed against him. Her hands grasped his shirt and she looked into his dark eyes, a small breath leaving her body as she felt his muscles twitch under the chambray. Sunshine, lye, and the faint scent of cedar washed over her as she inhaled. His eyes softened as he looked at her, his jaw still firm.

She wondered if he was as nervous as she was about marrying a stranger.

"T-t-thank you." She was starting to feel warm all over.

Staying in his embrace could be very dangerous.

She wanted to brush the dark hair away that swept over his forehead.

But she refrained.

She wondered if she could wrap the curl that was behind his ear around her finger.

But her hand remained still.

She longed to find out if his lips were as soft as they looked.

But she didn't lean forward.

Her eyes snapped back to his, grateful he couldn't read her thoughts.

"I won't ever let you fall," he said softly, his head moving towards her. His nostrils flared as his arm quickly went around her waist to prevent her from falling. He lowered her gently to the ground and his mouth thinned, making his lips almost invisible. Elizabet wondered if she had done something to upset him. "Where's the rest of your luggage?" he asked, stepping away from her.

Elizabet noticed the temperature drop immediately. How could one simple touch light her up like a bonfire at the end of harvest? She would need to be careful around Mr. Arkin. How she wished she had someone to talk to about the matters between men and women.

Lucinda mentioned briefly about the wedding night. That Elizabet should simply perform her wifely duty and lay as still as possible. Then it would be over without much discomfort. She noticed that Lucinda and Todd never touched each other. *Could that be how normal married couples behave?*

She wasn't even married yet, and she wanted to touch Mr. Arkin once more. Feel the steel of his arms hiding under the fabric. Wrap her hand in his large one just to feel the warmth. There would be no need for wood in the winter if she was that warm just from one simple touch.

"Your luggage, Miss Garrett?"

Realizing that Mr. Arkin was talking to her,

Elizabet shook the cobwebs from her head. "I don't have anything else. Just that one bag."

His handsome face contorted into a scowl. "That's it?"

Elizabet's cheeks flushed from embarrassment. "I didn't need much. And I don't have any household goods. Please," she pleaded. "Let's just go." She grasped his shirt sleeve. He gave her a quick nod and guided her to the wagon once more. "Oh," she said. "My flowers." She turned to gather the precious gift.

"Leave them," he said softly, a dangerous undertone returning to his voice. "I'll get you some more."

She glanced over her shoulder at Todd who hadn't moved from where he was kneeling on the ground, then allowed Mr. Arkin to help her onto the wagon seat. She moved over to the far side of the bench so he wouldn't have to walk around to climb in.

As she brushed the dust off her skirt, she noticed her intended approach Todd. The words were too low for her to hear, but the tone carried to her, tickling her ears. She would not want to be on the receiving end of whatever Mr. Arkin was saying to her brother right now.

Todd's face turned bright red, and his mouth opened as if he wanted to say something, but instead, he nodded then walked over to the wagon to Elizabet. "I'll let Lucinda know that you've left."

"Are you sure you won't change your mind about coming to the church?"

"I'm sure." His voice choked on the words. "Mr. Arkin will take real good care of you."

"Will you come to visit?"

Todd stepped back. "Not anytime soon. You need to get settled. We'll be busy with the young'un. When you are ready, let us know, and if it is convenient with your husband, we'll come to see you."

Elizabet nodded and watched as Todd moved back to the doorway. Mr. Arkin climbed in the wagon and with a flick of the reins, they rode out of the yard. She waited until they were past the field before turning to the driver. "Whatever did you say to him, Mr. Arkin?"

"I suppose you should call me Peter now that we are to be married."

"Alright, Peter." Elizabet shifted in her seat. "Are you going to tell me what you said to him?"

Peter wove the leather reins between his fingers and lifted his wooden leg, resting it on the buckboard upfront. "Nope. That's between me and him."

"Oh." She chewed on her bottom lip until it started to burn. "Do you think he meant he won't come out to visit?"

Peter shrugged. "He can come to visit you. I'm not going to keep you away from your family."

"But he said…"

"I know what he said." Peter put the reins in one hand and reached over to rub his leg. The fabric puckered where it caught on the edge of the wooden limb.

Elizabet looked around the wagon. "Did you bring your crutches?"

Peter glanced over at her. "Are you always this talkative?"

Giving a nervous laugh, she replied. "Not normally. I guess it is the nerves."

"So, Miss Garrett, tell me what you packed that you could fit it all in one small carpetbag."

"You should call me Elizabet."

"That's a right pretty name for a right pretty lady." Elizabet felt her ears turn red. No one ever called her pretty, before. "Your bag?" he prodded.

"Oh!" He must think her a simpleton if she kept losing track of her thoughts. She must not make it a habit. "Just a few things. I don't need much. I have a spare day dress, my apron. I brought my old boots." She turned and smiled at him. "Oh, and my Momma's

Bible. I thought we could teach our children to read by it…" her voice trailed off.

"I'd like that. My Ma taught my brother and me to read by the Bible."

"You have a brother?"

"Yes. His name's Lukas."

"Does he live around here?"

Peter dragged his hand down his face. "I don't know where he lives. After Ma died, he just packed up and left. Haven't seen him in about ten years."

Elizabet bit her fingernail, thinking about what he said. How difficult it must have been to have your only sibling leave you alone. It must have been just as difficult as having one invade your life.

"Do you want children, Mr. Arkin? I mean, Peter?"

"I'd like a few strapping boys. What man wouldn't? But I'd be happy with a girl that looks just like her Momma and can keep up with her brothers. How about you?"

"I'd like a large family. At least half a dozen."

Peter let loose a whistle. "That's quite a number."

"That way no one would ever be alone." Elizabet looked at the small town rising in the distance and wiped the tear that was threatening to appear from her eye.

"You alright?"

Elizabet nodded. "Just a bit of dust kicked up in my face." The lie was bitter on her tongue. "Is Marmee meeting us at the church?" Marmee and one of her daughters were serving as witnesses to the ceremony.

"She said she would."

The short distance to the church was traveled in silence and Elizabet tried to ignore the questions swirling in her head. When the small white building appeared in the distance, Marmee and a woman Elizabet didn't recognize were waiting on the steps for them to arrive. She gave a little wave and waited for the women to wave back before turning her gaze back to Peter.

Very shortly this man would be her husband. She closed her eyes and whispered a quick prayer that he would be kind, and for God to bless the marriage. She opened her eyes as she felt the wagon roll to a stop.

Peter pulled the brake on the wagon and tied the reins to the brake handle. "Ready?"

Her tongue felt thick, and her mouth was dry. How could she go from being perfectly fine to feeling like she wanted to retch? And how could Peter appear so collected?

She gave a little nod and wished she knew what he was thinking.

CHAPTER FOUR

"Ready?" Peter looked at the woman who, in a few moments was going to be his wife.

She nodded. He would have pulled up with her side closest to the church steps, but it was apparent that she didn't mind moving over on the bench, and right now he was grateful not to have to walk around the wagon.

He slid from the wagon bench and landed on the ground with a thud. The wooden leg jarred against his tender skin. Wincing, he made a note to pick up some horse liniment when he stopped by the mercantile before heading home.

Unfortunately, that wasn't all he would be picking up.

A single day dress, an apron, a pair of old boots

and her Momma's Bible.

If he could have pummeled Elizabet's brother into the ground, Peter would have. *One bag.* She had one bag with everything she owned inside.

It wasn't as if the house she lived in was lacking. They just chose to treat her … *less than.*

Peter knew Elizabet was a hard worker. He could tell by the calluses on her hands when she slipped her small hand in his larger one. Just as he wrapped his large hand around hers, he wanted to wrap his arms around her tiny frame and protect her from everything and everyone.

Starting with her brother.

When Todd bumped into Elizabet, knocking her to the ground, Peter wanted to roar and destroy the man that dare hurt the woman he was going to marry. It didn't matter that he didn't love her, or truly know her; no one was going to harm his family.

Now Elizabet was his responsibility. And he was going to make sure that she didn't want for anything. Turning, he held his arms open, and she gave a little jump from the wagon seat. And just as before, he held her for a moment longer than necessary. Her large green eyes looked at him, as he gently guided her down to the ground.

He saw her breath quicken as he held her arms.

Lips the color of ripe strawberries parted slightly, and the tip of her tongue peeked out from between rows of white teeth. Peter closed his eyes and reluctantly released her. When he opened them, she had moved away and was walking towards Marmee, and a woman with a rather large belly protruding from her day jacket.

Checking the brake once more, he tugged on his jacket and walked towards the ladies.

"Mrs. Chapman," he said, lifting his hat to Marmee and then offering a slight bow to the expecting mother. "Mrs. Chapman." Placing the hat back on his head, he turned to Elizabet. "Miss Garrett, this is Mrs. Pollyanna Chapman. She is married to Marmee's youngest son, Everett."

"How do you do?" Elizabet responded softly. "I don't believe I've met him."

"I am so glad I could be here today to watch you get married," Pollyanna said, handing a basket to Peter. Looking at his wooden foot, she pulled it back. "I'll put this in the back of the wagon. We made you a wedding supper so you wouldn't have to cook. There is ham, fried chicken, biscuits, boiled eggs, and sponge cake."

Marmee laughed. "Pollyanna is an excellent baker. I keep saying she needs to open a shop here in town."

"Thank you so much. Here," Elizabet said, offering to take the basket from Pollyanna, "let me take that. I'll put it in the back of the wagon."

"I can do it, Bet," Peter said.

She paused, her arms still outstretched and blinked several times. She reminded Peter of the owl that nested in the barn. "Bet?" She shook her head as if clearing cobwebs from the corners. "It is going to take a few minutes for you to get up the stairs," she said softly. "You get started and I'll be right there to help you."

"I don't need help." He must have said it harsher than he intended as her chin dropped and she turned away.

"Of course. I didn't mean anything by it."

Peter watched as she walked towards the wagon with Pollyanna. He felt Marmee's eyes drilling into him. "What?" he demanded.

Shrugging her shoulders, Marmee started up the stairs. "Nothing. Are you coming?"

Peter lifted his wooden foot and used it to brace himself as he lifted his healthy leg up the step. "Yeah. I'm coming."

"Where's her brother and sister-in-law?"

He found it interesting that Marmee referred to

Elizabet's relatives as brother and sister-in-law, where there was no delineation between sons, daughters and in-laws in the Chapman household. They were simply a family.

Peter winced as he took the next step. "They aren't coming. I don't think her brother approved of the wedding."

"Hmmm. The preacher already arrived and is waiting inside."

"I got her flowers," he blurted out.

"Flowers?"

Peter nodded. "For a bouquet. They were dropped, I didn't get a chance to find any others."

Marmee smiled. "I'm sure we can find something. You keep going and I'll be right back." She took off down the steps two at a time, lifting her skirt so she could jump over the steps.

"Where's she going?" Elizabet asked, joining Peter on his step. He hadn't progressed very far.

"She had to go get something." He stiffened his leg and climbed another step.

"How's your leg feeling?"

"Hurts like the dickens." He glanced at Elizabet who was keeping pace with him. "You can go ahead if you want."

"No need. I'll stay with you."

They climbed the last few steps in silence. She stayed next to him the entire way, stepping ahead of him, and then waiting for him to position his leg and push himself up to the next step. There was no censure or condemnation in her face as she patiently waited for him to make the climb up the seven steps to the church entrance.

By the time they reached the door to the church his leg was throbbing, and he regretted his choice of leaving his crutches at home. He could feel his skin tearing with each step and he winced with each step towards the altar.

"Did you bring a witness?" Reverend Billings asked, waving them forward. The reverend was a younger man, recently replacing Reverend O'Brien who had retired.

As they approached the first pew, Elizabet motioned for him to sit. "Mrs. Chapman is coming. Can you prepare us for what we need to do? I'm afraid I must get my husband home as quickly as possible after the service."

"Are you unwell, Peter?" Concern was evident in the Reverend's voice. "Perhaps we should delay the ceremony?"

Absolutely not! If they delayed, it meant that

Elizabet would have to go back home to her brother and his wife. There was no way he would send that gentle woman back there.

He was firm in his words to Todd Garrett.

She's your sister now, but in a few hours, she will be my wife. As my wife, I will protect her with every breath in my body. You are to never make her upset again or to do anything that might cause her harm. Do I make myself clear?

"Peter?" Elizabet's melodic voice broke through his thoughts. He would do anything in his power to protect her.

Peter shook his head, dismissing the unpleasant thoughts from earlier and smiled at the preacher. "I apologize. I just overexerted myself. Please, let's continue."

"Ah," Reverend Billings said. "Here are the Mrs. Chapmans."

"Flowers for the bride," Marmee said, handing the flowers to Peter.

"These are for you," he murmured to Elizabet. "Marmee picked out some beautiful ones to replace the ones that were dropped."

"They are beautiful." She took the offered flowers and pulled them to her nose. "Thank you, Peter.

Flowers, twice in one day. Imagine that." Peter was pleased he made her happy.

"Are you ready?" The reverend motioned for Peter and Elizabet to take their places at the front of the altar.

Peter repeated the words the preacher spoke, and when it came time, he pulled a ring from his vest pocket. "This was my mother's ring," he said softly as he slipped a plain gold band over her knuckle. "My parents were very happy. I hope we can be happy together."

Elizabet gave a little smile and Peter felt his heart skip a beat. "I'd like that," she whispered. She reached a hand up and gently wiped the perspiration away that was dotting his brow. "We'll get you home quickly so you can put your leg up."

When the reverend pronounced them man and wife, Peter leaned down and cupping her face with his hands, he pressed his lips to hers. Instantly all thoughts of the pain in his leg disappeared and his brain was consumed with the pleasure of the kiss. He heard her breath hitch as he claimed her as his wife.

Her hands made their way to his shoulders and her fingers curled around them, her nails pressing through the fabric of his vest. Peter blocked out everything but the feel of the softness beneath him and the pressure of her hands against his shoulders.

Elizabet pressed against Peter's shoulders, pushing him away as the Reverend cleared his throat. Peter lifted his head, looking at her, a pink stain colored her cheeks. The sound of giggles carried over his shoulders.

"I think you'll do just fine," the reverend said. "Why don't we sign the register and then you can head home?"

After scrawling his name underneath Elizabet's, he thanked the reverend, made his excuses to Marmee and Mrs. Chapman, and hobbled towards the exit to the wagon waiting outside. He heard Elizabet talking to the Chapmans and then follow him. She placed her hand on his back as he took the steps slowly.

"You don't have to do that," he said sharply.

She removed her hand immediately. "I was only trying to help."

"I don't need your help; I can do it on my own."

"Of course."

They made it to the wagon in silence. She didn't say anything as she climbed up the wheel and scooted to the far side of the bench. It only took several tries for him to pull himself up in the wagon and rest his leg on the buckboard.

He could barely look at her. He knew this wasn't a

love match. She told him exactly why she needed to get married, and he let her know exactly what he expected of his wife. Now that they were married, he wondered if he regretted kissing her the way he did. He wondered if he regretted the words he spoke as he slipped the ring on her finger.

No, he didn't regret that.

He prayed they could be happy. If they couldn't be in love, they could at least be comfortable with each other. That would be enough. Wouldn't it?

"Peter?" she asked. "Are you alright?"

He nodded. Failure wracked every bone in his body.

She deserved more than a man who could walk for no more than a few steps.

His jaw hurt from clenching his teeth. She didn't deserve his terse words. "I'm sorry for being short."

"You are in pain. I would be grumpy as well. Let's just go home."

"We need to stop by the mercantile."

"Whatever for? You need to get home and put your leg up."

"I don't get to town that often. I need to take advantage of the trip."

"Can't we come out later in the week?"

Peter shook his head. "I can't be away from the farm for that long."

"But you don't—"

"Just because I only have one leg, it doesn't mean I can't oversee my farm."

"I didn't mean to imply…"

"I know, Bet. Let's just get going. Yaw," he said, slapping the horse's rump with the reins. It only took a few minutes before they arrived in front of the mercantile.

"Do you have a list?" Elizabet asked, stepping down from the wagon. "I can fetch the items and you sit here and rest your leg."

Peter lifted his wooden leg and swung it over the side of the wagon, easing himself down to the ground. "No. I left it at home." He hated lying to her, but he wasn't planning on making this trip until he saw her threadbare carpetbag.

He hobbled to the mercantile door, and grimaced as he saw the bench where just yesterday, he was waiting for the stage to arrive. Holding the door open, he waved Elizabet inside the large store. It was filled with every type of sundry someone would need for living so remotely. The Ardens had supplies delivered weekly on one of the stagecoaches, so if they didn't have something in stock, they could get it in short order. Larger items were delivered by wagon train that would pass by the small town once a month.

"Mr. Arkin!" Rose said, coming from around the counter. "What brings you in here today? I thought you were set for supplies."

"Just need a few things, Rose," he responded, leaning down to rub his knee. "Do you happen to have a seat around?"

"Dillon!" she called. A middle-aged man popped his head out from behind a curtain. "Can you grab a stool for our friend?" She turned to smile at Peter. "He'll be right out. Now what were you looking for?"

Dillon Arden appeared with a wooden stool that he sat next to the counter. "Here you go, Peter. You can lean against this while I get whatever you need. Turns out we had seeds come on the stage yesterday."

"Seeds? The wheat should seed itself this winter." Peter sat down on the stool as his eyes glanced around the shop to spy Elizabet looking over items under an apothecary sign.

"Nah. Rose got it in her fool head to order flower seeds from back East."

"Flower seeds?"

"Yeah. Saw them in a catalog last winter. Put the order in and promptly forgot all about them. I guess they finally arrived. Now what am I going to do with all these flower seeds?"

"I dunno. I'm sure someone will want them." He watched as Elizabet picked up several jars and twisted the tops off them, bringing them up to her nose. His lips curled into a smile as she grimaced upon inhaling whatever potion was contained in the glass pots.

"What brings you in today," Dillon asked, repeating his wife's question.

"Do you have any dresses?"

"I never pegged you for the dress wearin' type, Mr. Arkin," Rose snickered.

Peter glared at her. "They are for my wife."

"Elizabet? You married Elizabet?"

Peter ignored Rose's question. "She needs at least two already made and enough fabric for two more. Plus, any undergarments. A pair of sturdy boots and anything else she needs."

"Oh my," Rose said, lifting her fingers to her mouth. "That's quite a bit." She hurried over to where Elizabet was still rifling through jars on the counter. Rose must have mentioned what Peter said as Elizabet turned to look at him.

He nodded to her and pointed towards the rack of dresses in the corner of the shop before turning to

Dillon. "Add her to my account for any future purchases she needs if she comes to town without me."

"Do you need anything else?" Dillon pulled a ledger from the drawer and opened it before scribbling on a page. Slamming the ledger closed, he placed it back in the drawer.

"Liniment."

"Red or white?"

"Red." The pepper would sting like the dickens, but it would soothe his aching muscles. "That's all." He placed his elbow on the counter and closed his eyes, listening to the sounds in the store and praying it wouldn't be long before he could get his wife home.

CHAPTER FIVE

"Peter?" Elizabet reached out and gently shook Peter's arm.

His head fell with a *thunk* and he jumped in his seat, his wooden boot scraping against the floor as he tried to right himself. *Poor man*, she thought. *He must be exhausted.*

"Wh-what?" Peter shook his head and looked around the mercantile. "I'm sorry, Bet. How long was I asleep?"

"Not long at all. You just drifted off. Five minutes at the most." She held a dress in her hand. "Mrs. Arden only had one dress that would fit. I don't want you to spend your money on me."

"Nonsense," he spat. She flinched as the word carried over curled lips. "I'm not going to have you wearing rags. I'm not your brother. You're my wife. I'll take care of you. Are you sure there aren't any others?"

She shook her head. "No," she choked on the word.

He must have seen the tears burning in her eyes as he reached out to gently catch her arm. "I'm not upset with you, Bet. I just want you to be properly outfitted." He softened his voice. "If there aren't any more dresses, order one. But let's get fabric and you can make another dress. You can sew, can't you?" Elizabet nodded. "That's my girl. Pick out something pretty. I see a yellow fabric with blue flowers over there. That would look mighty pretty on you."

"Peter, we really need to get you home," Elizabet insisted. "These items can wait until we come back to town."

"It might be a month, Bet."

"Then it is a month. I'll get this dress, the fabric, and some notions. Anything else can wait."

She saw Peter press his lips into a thin line, but he nodded. Reaching out to give his arm a quick squeeze, she smiled. "I'll be right back, so we can get home." She placed the dress on the counter, her fingers lingering on the lace. She had never had a dress so fine. Mrs. Arden was already cutting the yellow and blue fabric when Elizabet made her way to the far counter.

"I heard what Peter said," Mrs. Arden offered. "It is a beautiful fabric. I think three yards will be plenty. Do you want any lace for the cuffs or collar?"

"No. But I'll take some plain linen for a caplet."

"He wanted you to get enough for two dresses. And undergarments."

"Then add more linen and I can make a work dress from this." She placed dark blue calico with white dots on the counter. "I'll need thread and needles. I don't have any."

Mrs. Arden pointed to a display of notions and then started to measure folds from the darker bolt of fabric.

Elizabet placed several spools of thread on the counter and a small pack of needles. Todd had never allowed her to make her own purchases, and Lucinda certainly never let her pick out anything from the mercantile. It was a new feeling. One that Elizabet liked, but she didn't want to take advantage of Peter's generosity. She smiled with the giddiness of it all.

Mrs. Arden scribbled on a piece of paper. "I'll get these wrapped, but you can take this to the counter and my husband will ring you up."

"Have I forgotten anything?"

The shopkeeper's wife looked at the small pile.

"Buttons?"

"Oh," Elizabet laughed. "Just plain ones for now. And I'll need a piece of chalk."

Adding two cards to the pile, Mrs. Arden scribbled on the piece of paper. "You can get the chalk at the register. Tell Mr. Arden I've put it on here. Anything else?"

Elizabet looked over at the balms in the apothecary section. "I'd like one of those jars of that Wonder Jelly. But I'd like to pay for it separately, please."

Mrs. Arden raised her eyebrow. "Do you want to pay for it at the counter?"

Elizabet shook her head. "No. I'll just pay you, if you don't mind." She didn't want Peter seeing the purchase, she hoped that she would be able to surprise him. "The sign said twenty-five cents?" She placed three coins in Mrs. Arden's hand and picked up a small box, placing it in her reticule. Taking the paper from Mrs. Arden, she made her way to the register.

Peter was talking to Mr. Arden about the price of wheat as she placed the paper on a brown package tied with string in front of him. "Mrs. Arden is wrapping everything up," she said softly.

Mr. Arden took the paper and quickly added up the figures. "Ten dollars and seventy-three cents."

Elizabet let out a gasp and quickly pressed her fingers to her lips. She didn't want to embarrass Peter in front of the shopkeeper. Peter rummaged in his pocket and pulled out several crumpled bills and placed them on the counter.

"Rose should be done wrapping your packages shortly, Mrs. Arkin."

Mrs. Arkin. She knew she was married, but to hear someone else call her that. She wanted to beam with pride. She vowed to be a good wife to Peter. And that meant getting him home.

"Thank you. Peter, why don't you go to the wagon. I can bring the packages along."

Peter's brow wrinkled. "I can…"

"I know you can. But let me help, husband."

Peter paused and stared at her with soft brown eyes. He nodded and waved to the shopkeeper before slowly making his way to the door. Once he was outside, Elizabet picked up her packages. "Thank you for your help."

"Mrs. Arkin?" The shopkeeper called to her.

Elizabet turned. "Yes?"

"I think you'll be very good for him."

"I hope we'll be good for each other. Good day, Mr. and Mrs. Arden." Elizabet juggled the packages and followed her husband to the wagon. Peter had already climbed into the wagon and his foot was resting on the buckboard. Securing the packages behind her satchel, she climbed up beside him. "Ready to go?"

Peter gave the horse a light slap and they were off towards the edge of town. "I'm sorry I wasn't much use back there."

"Don't apologize." Elizabet looked at the buildings as they made their way down the main street through town. In a few moments they passed the last wooden structures and were looking at the open prairie. "How far is it to your home?"

"Our home," he gently corrected. "About an hour ride."

"That's probably why you don't come to town much." Elizabet bit her bottom lip. "Thank you for purchasing those things for me today. You didn't need to."

"You said that in the store."

She shifted in her seat. "I guess I did. I've never had a new dress."

"Never?"

Elizabet shook her head. "No. Lucinda would get new clothes. I'd get her dresses that she didn't like or that were worn."

"She's not as tall as you."

"No. I'd just add more fabric to the bottom, so the skirts didn't look so awkward."

"She's also larger than you."

"It's easier to take a dress in, than to let it out."

Peter emitted a low growl. It reminded Elizabet of the mountain lions that would sometimes get too close to the ranch.

"Are you alright?" she asked.

He tightened his grip on the reins, veins bulging from the back of his hands. "I'm just thinking."

"Good thoughts?" she asked, hopefully.

Peter released his grip, the veins relaxing under his skin. He gave an uncomfortable laugh. "Are you always so cheerful?"

She lifted her shoulders. "I guess I am. There really isn't much to be unhappy about." Looking at the wooden boot resting on the buckboard she grimaced. "I'm sorry, I didn't mean…"

"I know you didn't."

"I think things happen for a reason."

"You do?"

"Of course. If you hadn't lost your leg, you

wouldn't have asked Mrs. Chapman to help you. If Lucinda hadn't been insisting on my finding somewhere else to live, I wouldn't have sought help from Mrs. Chapman. If that woman on the stage hadn't been what she was…"

"That's a lot of ifs, Bet."

"But it brought us together."

Peter looked out at the landscape thoughtfully. "I guess it did."

"Peter?"

He turned to look at her. "What is it, Bet?"

She liked the way his name rolled off her tongue. It sounded slow like molasses in January, but warm like a cup of Marmee's hot apple cider. Looking at him from beneath thick lashes, she gave him a little smile.

"I was wondering if you should take off your leg."

Peter scrambled to secure the reins that fell from his hand and slid across the buckboard as he listened to Elizabet's question.

Maybe he underestimated his new bride.

Weaving the reins between his fingers he tightened his fist, the leather digging into his skin. He would not make that mistake again.

Peter looked at her and lifted his eyebrow. Elizabet laughed. "I guess that does sound rather ridiculous. I was just thinking that if it hurt that much, you could at least ease your pain for the journey home."

"I'll leave my leg right where it is."

"May I ask how you hurt yourself?"

Peter cleared his throat. "Why all these questions?" He tried not to sound annoyed with her, but for mercy's sake she was a talkative one.

He watched as she turned away from him and looked out on the prairie. "I just wanted to know more about you. I figured since we were married, you know. Don't you have any questions for me?"

"No. I don't." He slapped the reins lightly, urging the horse to pick up speed. Peter stayed silent as the wagon rocked along the dry road.

It wasn't long before they crested a small hill and his farm came in view.

"What are those?" Elizabet asked, pointing to black dots in the distance.

"Those are beef cattle," Peter explained. "Most of them belong to the Chapmans. Their house is over there." He pointed towards the east, where the creek wound around a clump of trees. "Weston feeds his cattle on my land during the winter months and during the summer, they are set out to that range to pasture."

"You don't own any cows?"

Peter chuckled. "Those aren't cows. They are steers. A might nasty too, if you get close. I had planned on raising beef cattle. This land is perfect for it, but after the … well, let's just say I don't have the strength to be riding a horse all day and rounding up strays."

"So how do you make a living?"

Peter scrubbed his chin. "You don't think I can support you? I heard what your brother said."

"No." Elizabet twisted her hands in her lap. Peter knew she was lying. A lie of omission was just as bad as an outright fib.

"But you are worried."

"I'd be lying if I said I wasn't."

He guided the wagon towards the small barn at the edge of the property. "I own my farm and all the land around it. Nearly five hundred acres. My brother and I purchased it outright. I'll show you around tomorrow, but that's the house, and there is a garden around the side. It hasn't been worked in nearly a year, so it is overgrown. There is a field of wheat that Weston will harvest this fall. I have chickens and a milking cow."

"You work all this yourself?"

"Weston rents the land. That is how I make my living. He has workers that come and plant and harvest. And he rents the fields to pasture his steers. It means I don't have to worry, and I don't have to sell. I make a good enough living to support you, Bet."

She gave a hesitant smile. "I like it that you call me Bet. My brother called me Lizzy, but I like your nickname better." Why was she suddenly nervous?

Peter pulled outside the barn. "I need to put the horse away and then I'll come to the house. Why don't you go inside?"

"I'll help you." Before he could refuse, she placed her hand on his arm and he felt a calming unlike any he had known before. He knew he wasn't alone. She gave his arm a quick squeeze and hopped down from the wagon. "Are you going to just leave the wagon here?"

He swallowed; the words jumbled in his brain. It was a simple question, why was he having difficulty answering it? It was because he never had anyone offer to sincerely help. Marmee was different. She came barging in and took over. Elizabet was here because she wanted to be. *He hoped.*

"Peter?"

Her voice broke through his thoughts. "Yes. I used to put it in the building over there, but it was too much work to put it in and out, so I just leave it here."

Elizabet walked over to the small structure attached to the side of the barn. It was large enough for a wagon to be stored, but not long enough for both the wagon and horse. The farmer would have to unhitch the horse and then manually pull the wagon into the structure.

"If you take out the back wall you could drive straight through," she called to him.

"Excuse me?" Peter pulled his leg from the buckboard and lowered it off the side of the wagon before jumping down.

Elizabet walked back towards the wagon. "I said, if you removed the back of the shed, you could drive the wagon straight through. Then unhitch the horse at the other end. Then when you needed to leave, just hitch the horse back up and drive out of the shed." She moved over to the side of the horse and started tugging on the harness. "It would make things easier on you."

Peter hobbled to the front of the horse and pulled the reins over the animal's head. "You really are something, Miss Garrett."

"Mrs. Arkin. My name is Mrs. Arkin." She

glanced over the backside of the horse at him, her eyes crinkling at the edges. "There. All done. Let's get him watered and fed and then we can do the same for you." She giggled at her words and the laughter rushed over Peter like the sweetest of melodies.

He definitely underestimated her.

CHAPTER SIX

Elizabet insisted that Peter sit near the workbench while she watered and fed the horse. He put up a bit of a fuss, but then backed down, when she nearly pushed him into the seat. She giggled at the thought of a woman of her small stature bossing around the tall farmer, but he finally complied, and she was able to lead the horse into the stall.

"What's his name?" she asked as she removed the last of the accoutrements and handed them to Peter. "I can't call him Horse."

"I didn't name him. I guess I didn't name any of the animals." Peter laid the tack on the workbench. "The oats are over there, and the water pump is right outside the barn door. I can get the water."

"No," Elizabet insisted, pouring a scoop of oats in a bucket attached to the post. "I need to learn everything."

"It's your wedding day, Bet."

Was that a growl in his voice?

"Well, it's your wedding day too, Peter, so let's just get this done and we can go inside and get dinner." Annoyed at fighting with him, she knew he was tired, but why didn't he just do something about it? It wasn't her fault he left his crutches at home. Rubbing her brow, she picked up the bucket. "In fact, why don't you head towards the house, and I'll be right along."

She lifted her chin and strode past him towards the barn door, to the water pump she could see just outside. As her skirt brushed his leg, she felt his arm snake around her waist and pull her close to him.

"Elizabet," he whispered, pressing his face into her back. He inhaled deeply. "Don't get upset. That isn't the way to start off our marriage. I'm just frustrated that I can't do everything I want... I need to do."

Dropping the bucket, she turned in his arms and removed his hat, tossing it over his shoulder onto the workbench.

"That's so I can look at you," she said softly. His untamed hair curled around his ears as her fingers hesitantly reached out and touched one of the strands.

Even though he had shaved earlier, already the scruff of a shadow appeared on his chin. "I don't *need* you to do anything for me, other than provide a home for me and our children. Protect us, make sure we have enough to eat and that we are safe."

"Maybe your brother was right. That I'm less of a man." He turned his face away.

"Peter," she mimicked his growl. Using two fingers she lifted his chin. "It takes a special man to do what you did. You knew you needed a helpmate. You asked Mrs. Chapman to help you and I can't get over everything you did today. Standing up to my brother, bringing me flowers... not once, but twice. Buying me those beautiful clothes. I've never had anything new in my entire life. If anything, you are more than a man."

Without thought or hesitation, she leaned down and gently pressed her lips to his. She felt his hand trace up her back and stop at the nape of her neck, pulling her closer to him. The whiskers breaking through his skin tickled her cheeks as she gripped his head firmly. Heat rose in her cheeks as he deepened the kiss, claiming her as his own.

Breathless, she pulled away.

What must he think? He gazed at her with hooded eyes, a tired smile creeping on his lips.

"I'm sorry, Peter," she began.

"I'm not," he gave a light laugh.

"You're not?"

He pulled her tighter. "You can kiss me anytime. It stopped my leg hurting."

Elizabet put her hands on his shoulders and pressed another quick kiss against his lips. "Not hurting?"

"Nope."

"Good," she giggled. "Let me get the horse watered and you can carry the packages."

He reluctantly let her go. "It might be hurting again. I might need another kiss."

Elizabet picked up the bucket and leaned forward, her eyes closed and her lips puckered in great exaggeration. Peter laughed heartily and she felt his hand cup her chin and press a kiss against her lips with a loud smack.

"I'm going to go water the horse now," Elizabet said, flouncing towards the barn door. Peter followed and stood by the wagon as she filled the bucket and watered the horse. "Do I need to do anything else?"

"Not right now. I'll brush him later when I milk the cow."

"I can come back and help."

Peter didn't say anything. He reached in the back

of the wagon and passed Elizabet the basket filled with treats from Marmee. "I'll carry the packages and the carpetbag." He put them on the edge of the wagon before balancing them in his arms.

Elizabet hooked the basket on her arm and took two of the packages, pressing them against her chest. She raised her eyebrow, daring Peter to say anything. He silently picked up the remaining packages and the carpetbag before walking across the yard.

As they strolled towards the small farmhouse, Elizabet had a chance to look around. The garden area was overgrown, and she spied chickens darting between the foliage gobbling up grasshoppers and locust.

"Where's the chicken house?"

"Chicken house?"

"Yes. Where do the chickens lay their eggs?"

Peter shuffled the packages to free his hand, allowing him to scratch his head. "I don't know. I find some in the barn. I guess they go in there at night."

"You don't have an actual coop?"

"I did, but we had a bad storm, and I haven't gotten around to rebuilding it."

"Hmm."

She looked at the exterior of the house. It was two

stories but didn't appear very large from the outside. It was solidly made from wooden boards that had been painted at one time. It needed to be painted again, she noted, as large flakes of faded paint fell to the ground under the harsh sun. Mortar made from mud mixed with grass, straw and moss filled the cracks and corners. Four large glass windows gazed upon them as they approached the three steps leading up to a sturdy porch.

It was a fine house other than lacking a woman's touch and needing a new coat of paint, but it was hers.

"I'm afraid it is rather simple inside. I've not done much since the accident."

"I'm sure it will be just fine," she grinned. "I can't wait to see inside. Let me get the door since your hands are full." She moved ahead of him and lifted the latch, pushing the door open.

"Go inside and put the basket on the table. I'm right behind you."

Elizabet stepped across the threshold. She gave a little sigh. How often she dreamed of being carried across the threshold of her new home as a bride. Glancing back at Peter, she knew that it was selfish of her to think of such romanticism. Her husband was more than enough.

She was away from Lucinda; she was married to

an honorable man, and she had a home to call her own.

She didn't need to worry about what she didn't have.

The smoky smell of charred wood infused the damp air inside the house. Apparently, the windows hadn't been open in a while. That would be the first thing she rectified.

Looking at the windows, she discovered there weren't any curtains to block the morning sun. *There was the second.*

Near the door was a wooden table with two chairs, a mason jar filled with the same type of flowers Peter brought to her at the church sat in the middle of the table. Elizabet rested the basket on the edge of the table and slid the packages next to it. Fingering the flowers, she smiled and peered around the rest of the room and her smile quickly faded.

There wasn't much to look at and Elizabet tried her best to hide her disappointment. The room was sparsely furnished. A stuffed mattress with a quilted coverlet lay on the floor against one wall. A rocker, a footstool and a small table with woodworking tools sat near a brick fireplace. Pieces of unfinished furniture scattered about the large hearth. Noticing a large arm that would be used to allow a pot to rest over the flames while cooking, Elizabet allowed her eyes to glance around the rest of the room. *There wasn't a stove!*

She hadn't cooked over an open fire in years. A cast-iron bread oven sat waist high in the brick wall, which would make cooking easier. At least she wouldn't have to worry about covering an oven with hot coals.

Despite the ash covering the sparse furnishing, the house had potential. In the corner farthest from the fireplace, a set of stairs disappeared behind a recessed wall. She wondered what was upstairs if the bed was downstairs in the open room. There was also a standing cupboard and a small doorway.

Taking off her hat, she draped it on the chair and turned to Peter.

"Let me show you around," he said, as he placed the carpetbag on the floor. Turning on his good leg, he held his arms open wide. "This is it. Welcome to your new home."

"It's…" she tried to think of the appropriate words that wouldn't offend him. "It's rather large in here."

Peter's eyes scanned her face. "You're disappointed?"

She shook her head. "I guess I expected furniture." She waved her hand around the room. "And a stove. But those are silly things given we have a roof over our heads."

"No. They aren't." Peter ran his hand down his face. "I've been alone for so long, I guess I really didn't think about how it might look to a lady."

"Is that what you think of me, Peter? A lady?"

"Of course, Bet." She giggled and he furrowed his brow, creases appearing across his handsome face. "What are you laughing about?"

"Could you imagine that hoity-toity miss coming out here and seeing this?"

"Madeline?"

"Was that her name? The one with the big feather?" Elizabet raised her hand in the air as if pushing the imaginary object away.

Peter thought about it for a moment and then laughed. "I think this may have just done her in." He pulled out a chair. "I do need to get some weight off this leg, though. If you don't mind."

"Oh, of course. Where are your crutches?" She moved the picnic basket to the other side of the table and walked the packages over to the mattress on the floor. She spied the crutches leaning in the dark corner near the fireplace, along with several single shoes, lined up neatly in a row.

Picking them up, she returned to see that Peter was

sitting with his leg under the table. His hands were moving and then the wooden leg fell to the floor with a thud. He breathed a sigh of relief. "Just leave it. I'll get it in a minute."

Elizabet walked by and leaned the crutches against the wall. She could see the perspiration dotting her husband's forehead. She wasn't sure what to do. "Peter?" The color had drained from his face. "Do you need a doctor?"

He shook his head. "No. I just need a minute."

Elizabet reached down to pick up the wooden leg. It was heavy and smooth, made from wood, iron, and leather. No wonder it weighed so much! It was worn in places from where Peter had leaned on it as he walked. There was a joint at the knee, secured with iron fittings which allowed for slight movement. At the top, a leather brace which would go behind Peter's leg held a strap with a buckle that would secure around his leg, and led into a leather cup that would support his limb.

Elizabet noticed the leather was dark and slightly damp. When she rubbed her thumb across it, streaks of red colored her skin.

"Peter, you are bleeding."

CHAPTER SEVEN

Peter watched as Elizabet rubbed the blood between two fingers. He closed his eyes for a moment. He didn't want her to see him like this. He knew at some point she would see him, but not this way. Not now.

He'd rather give her time to get used to being around him before even seeing the reality that was his tangled limb. Or what was left of it.

His hand went down to his trouser leg, and he could feel the skin peek through the split fabric of his pants. Wincing as his fingers brushed against the raw skin, a rush of pain raced up his leg so quickly he braced himself against the table lest he lose control of his facilities.

"It's no bother, Bet. It's just where the leg rubs my skin."

"Let me see your leg." She put the boot next to the crutches and knelt on the ground next to him. Her head brushed against his hand, and he clenched it into a fist as to not reach out and stroke her hair.

"No. I'll take care of it." He moved his hand to block her from viewing the puckered flesh.

"I insist." She brushed his hand aside. "Let me help you. That's what I'm here for." Tugging on his pant leg, she stopped when the fabric split apart along the seam. There was a discrete row of hook and eyes sewn along the seam of the pants. This allowed him to put on his pants, then his prosthesis and fasten his pant leg around it. "This is incredible," she said, fingering the hooks. "Did you think of this?"

"No. The man who was fixing my pants suggested it after I had ruined half a dozen pairs of pants. There were so many patches on them, the tailor couldn't repair them anymore. He thought it would be easier to modify the one leg."

"Is it?" Her green eyes looked up at him.

"It does help. I have pairs of pants that I wear when I use my crutches. It is easier to just fold and pin the fabric on those."

"It's brilliant." She pulled apart the seam and could see the angry skin where his leg once was. "Oh Peter," she whispered. "We need to get this cleaned up. It looks sore. How long has it been like this?"

"Well, since I lost my leg."

"I meant the raw skin. Did it never heal?" She blew on it slightly and Peter jumped. Her breath was soft and cool against his scorching flesh.

She could see bumps form on his flesh, the same type that would form on her arms in the cold, but it was warm outside.

"Yes, but the prosthetic rubs it. That's why I don't normally use it. It isn't like I gotta gussy up for the steers or the chickens. Old Bessie doesn't mind if I'm missing a leg."

"I thought you didn't name the animals." She looked at him from beneath her lashes.

"I guess I named her."

She wrapped her hands around the puckered flesh and Peter clamped his tongue between his teeth to prevent from crying out. "Am I hurting you?"

It wasn't pain in the way she imagined. Just having her hands touching his flesh made heat of a different type race through him. "No," he managed to spit out.

Oblivious to his discomfort, she continued to examine where the wood and leather rubbed his skin. "It isn't hot, which is good. It is just as you said. Let's get it cleaned up and I think you should let it air out and dry up." She rolled back on her heels. "Where's a bowl or a bucket?"

"In the cabinet." He pointed near the stairs.

"I remember when my brother fell off his horse," she called over her shoulder as she made her way to the cabinet. "Darn thing dragged him forever. All the skin on his back was plumb torn up. He had to sleep on his belly without a shirt, or a sheet so it could dry out. Doc said that would help the healing."

He heard the cabinet open, and her rummage through the contents. There wasn't much in there. Just a bowl, a small bag of rags, a bar of soap, a straight razor, and a looking glass. Elizabet's footsteps resonated across the wooden floor and she placed the bowl, soap and two rags on the table.

"Water's outside," Peter offered.

Without a word, she left to fill the small bowl. When she returned, she knelt by his side again and placed the bowl on the floor. As she reached for the soap and rags, Peter flexed his hand several times. He couldn't help himself. His fingers reached out and he stroked the soft strands of her golden locks.

"You have such pretty hair, Bet. It is the color of summer wheat."

Color spread over her cheeks. He forgot she wasn't used to such compliments, and he made a promise to compliment her every day. She ignored his words and got to work gently washing the skin and then rinsing it with clean water. The skin appeared less angry as the cool water ran down the limb into the bowl. Gently patting it dry, she looked up as if just remembering something important.

"Do you see my reticule on the table?"

He spied it on the far side of the table. Leaning over, he grabbed it with two fingers and passed it to her. "What would you need from in there?"

She tugged on the threads that held her reticule tight and once they were loose, she pulled out a small box and held it up to him. "Mrs. Arden said this just arrived. All the way from Pennsylvania. Can you imagine?"

"What is it?"

"It's called Wonder Jelly. Look at all these wonderful things it can do." She tore the top of the box off and dropped a small glass jar into her hand. "Benefits all bumps, sores, bruises, burns, blisters, cuts, and chafed skin. Mrs. Arden said that these factory workers were using petroleum to grease the rods in the machines, and this was some sort of after-product. Turns out the workers slathered it on their hands when they burned their skin and it caused it to heal faster." She finally took a deep breath and Peter tried not to laugh. "I'm talking too fast, aren't I? Todd always said when I get excited, I talk too fast."

"You purchased that for me?" His throat thickened as she nodded. "Wh-," he cleared his throat. "When?"

"When she was cutting fabric. I paid for it over there."

"You shouldn't have spent your money on me, Bet."

"You spent yours on me." She opened the jar and inhaled deeply. "It smells terrible, but it is supposed to work." She lifted the jar. "Want to sniff?"

Peter lifted his hands in mock surrender. "No. I trust you."

"You do?" She blinked rapidly.

"Yes. That it smells terrible."

Elizabet laughed and dug her finger into the jar. "Hold still. I don't know if this stings or not." She spread the greasy ointment over Peter's raw skin. "Does it hurt?"

He shook his head. The ointment soothed his skin almost immediately. The blackish ointment did have a unique scent, but Peter was grateful for the relief; and it didn't have the residual heat of the capsaicin liniment.

She capped the jar and placed it on the table before

wiping her finger with the dry rag. "I'll wash my hands and we can eat dinner."

Peter reached out and grabbed her arm. "Thank you. My leg feels much better." As he looked at her, he noticed her eyes soften. *Maybe, just maybe, she looked at him like a whole man?*

"I'm glad. Our vows said in sickness and in health. I will always take care of you."

Peter pressed a kiss against the back of her hand. The scent of the wonder jelly filled his nostrils. It wasn't as awful as Elizabet made it out to be. Rather, it was comforting. Pressing her hand against his cheek, he whispered against her skin. "You are a Godsend, Bet." He gave her hand a squeeze before releasing her.

As she walked outside to wash her hands and dump the water bowl, Peter closed his eyes and said a prayer of thanks for the first time since he lost his leg.

CHAPTER EIGHT

Elizabet hummed as she popped a large berry in her mouth, pausing only to savor the sweet flavor as it coated her tongue. She closed her eyes for a moment and chewed thoughtfully, and imagined the look of surprise on Peter's face when she made a blackberry cobbler for dessert.

They had been married for two days and they were the happiest of her entire life. Peter had crawled into the makeshift bed on the floor after dinner and fell promptly asleep. He did tell Elizabet that there was a bed upstairs that she could use, but Elizabet was having none of that.

What if her husband needed her?

So, she slipped underneath the covers and rolled on her side, letting Peter's gentle snores sing her to sleep. The following morning... *she blushed at the thoughts*.

There was nothing wrong with her husband. *Nothing*.

In her eyes, he was perfect. Her hand brushed gently over her day dress, and she prayed that soon she would be able to tell him that their family was growing.

Two days. She wondered how long it would take before she knew.

Perhaps she might ask the doctor the next time she went to town. Sighing heavily, she wished she had someone who taught her about those things growing up. Lucinda was absolutely no help at all.

Reaching into the metal bucket, she pulled out another berry and eyed it carefully before popping it into her mouth. She spied too many crawling creatures on the brambles to just chew unaware.

Tempted to eat another, she eyed her harvest carefully. If she devoured any more, there wouldn't be enough for a cobbler. She stopped by the barn and collected the afternoon eggs, gently placing them on top of the berries, before heading towards the house.

Peter was sitting on the porch with a man she didn't recognize. She raised her hand to shield her eyes from the sun, but still couldn't see who the stranger might be.

Looking down at her dress covered in blackberry juice, Elizabet bit her bottom lip. She didn't know they were expecting company, otherwise she might have postponed her berry-picking adventure.

Carefully approaching the porch, she noticed Peter's eyebrow raise as he took in her attire.

"You look like you had quite the adventure, Bet," Peter said with a slight humor.

Stopping at the bottom step, she grasped the bucket in both hands and wiggled her dirty toes that peeked out beneath her skirt. "I went blackberry picking by the creek." She eyed the stranger. "I thought I'd make a cobbler for dessert."

Peter leaned forward. "How many blackberries are left in the bucket?"

She narrowed her eyes and grinned at him. "Why do you ask?"

"Given your purple fingers, your stained lips and the color of your tongue, I'm wondering if there are enough to make dessert at all." He gave a laugh. "If there aren't, at least let me kiss you, to see if they are sweet."

"Peter!" Color flamed her cheeks. "You have company."

Peter held out his hand. "Bet, this is my brother, Lukas. He arrived after you left."

Elizabet jumped on the porch, ignoring the step. "Lukas? How wonderful. I know Peter must be so happy to have you back to visit. Are you staying in town? You will be staying for supper at least."

"Peter said you were a pistol," Lukas laughed. "I can see why you married her, brother."

"He married me…," her voice dropped. "Never mind. How long will you be in town, brother Lukas?"

Peter grabbed her arm and pulled her close to him, wrapping his arm around her hips. What was normally a tender touch, felt more possessive, as if he was claiming her in front of his brother.

Lukas scratched his chin. His hair was the same brown as his brother's, but the sun had bleached it in spots. "I dunno. I like moving from place to place. I thought I'd stay for a week or two, if you don't mind. You have some nice-looking cattle in that field over there."

"Those belong to my neighbor," Peter said.

"Do you know if he is hiring? Like extra hands?"

"I don't know."

"There is plenty of work here," Elizabet interrupted, "if you are looking for a job."

"Bet…"

"It's true, Peter. We could use the help."

"I can take care of my own."

Elizabet saw Lukas look at Peter's leg. "Would it be alright to stay in the barn?"

"Peter?" She wrapped her hand around her husband's shoulders and gave a little squeeze.

Peter reached his hand up and patted Elizabet's hand. "We have a room upstairs. After you left, I finished the house with only one room. You can use that. We sleep downstairs."

"I appreciate that, brother."

"I'm going to go inside and get these berries in a cobbler, then I'll get cleaned up. No point ruining another dress." She gave Lukas a smile. "I'm glad you are here." Looking at her husband, she brushed the hair away from his forehead. "Do you need anything?"

Pulling her down for a quick kiss, he released her and shook his head. "Nothing right now."

She went inside the house and put the bucket on the table. She put the eggs in one bowl and the berries in another. Covering the berries with water from a pitcher, she left them to soak for a bit while she went to wash her face and hands.

Humming softly, she filled the washbasin with the

remaining water and lathered a bar of soap, scrubbing the purple stains on her hands. She gasped as she caught a glimpse of herself in the mirror. She looked like an orphan.

No wonder Peter laughed when he saw her.

Her skin was colored from the sun and freckles were appearing on her nose. A streak of dirt went right across her forehead, there was a ring of blackberry juice around her lips. She looked like she was no more than a child!

Todd always told her to never go out without her bonnet. Why didn't she listen to him?

Lathering the soap with a fury, she washed her face until every spot of dirt and berry juice disappeared from her skin. She patted her face dry and moved the bowl to the floor. She'd take a bath later, but at least she would wash some of the dirt from her feet before dinner. By the time she was done the water was black as molasses.

Grimacing, she quickly dried her feet and put on day shoes and a clean apron before returning outside to dump the water over the side of the porch. Peter and his brother were engrossed in conversation, and she didn't want to interrupt.

Returning to her make-shift kitchen, she sorted the berries from the water and placed them in a third bowl where she added a bit of sugar. She listened to her husband's strong voice carry through the window as he talked to his brother. She didn't concentrate on the words, instead, just allowing the tone to wash over her as she completed preparing the cobbler for after supper, and then making a quick lunch as she knew the men must be hungry.

When she cleared the table, apart from a platter of thick ham sandwiches and a pitcher of cold lemonade, she went back to the porch. "Lunch is ready." She handed Peter his crutches and moved out of the way so he could maneuver into the house.

"Thank you, ma'am," Lukas said, following his brother.

"I made lemonade, but I can put on a fresh pot of coffee if you would prefer that."

"Lemonade is fine, Bet," Peter said. "Are you joining us?"

She shook her head. "I ate, while I was cleaning up. I'm going to go upstairs and get the room ready for Lukas. I've not had a chance to open the windows up there."

"I hope it's not a bother, ma'am."

Elizabet waved her arm. "It isn't. And call me Elizabet. I'm your sister now."

She walked by the dry sink and popped another berry in her mouth before she headed upstairs to see what she might find.

Peter listened to Elizabet's soft breathing as he stared at the ceiling. The room was hot and he wanted to kick off the covers, but he couldn't. He didn't have enough strength in his limb to push the coverlet off and if he kicked with his good leg, he risked kicking his wife. He rolled to his side and stuck his foot and ankle from beneath the covers, trying to cool down his body.

He didn't know if it was the summer heat or the fact that Bet was softly cooing in her sleep that had him hotter than a flapjack on a cast iron skillet. He pushed his leg out further and pulled up the leg of his underdrawers.

He didn't like the way Lukas looked at her. Not that his brother had done anything inappropriate. Not in the least.

His brother was honorable.

He was hardworking.

He made Elizabet laugh every moment since he arrived.

He was capable.

He helped shoe the horses.

He helped fix the leaking barn roof.

He carried wood for the fire so Elizabet could cook.

He even suggested creating an outdoor fireplace so it wouldn't be as warm in the house.

He was whole.

Lukas had both of his legs, and no amount of self-talk was going to change that.

Peter needed to admit. *He was jealous.*

Lukas had been with them for not even a week and Peter wanted him gone.

There was no reason for how he was feeling, but it churned in him like a cider fermenting. Soon it would be vinegar, and nothing could be done to turn it back to its original form.

Elizabet. His sweet Elizabet had been every inch of the proper wife.

She had kept the promises she made to Peter, ensuring his house was a home. She read the Bible to them every evening. She made him delicious meals. She uncovered the garden beneath all the weeds, milked the cow, repaired the chicken coop, and she didn't neglect his leg.

She wouldn't dare tend to him in front of his brother, but after Lukas went to bed, he waited with anticipation as she unwrapped his limb and gently bathed it before coating it in what she called *wonder jelly*.

He treasured those moments when it was just them and he could run his fingers through her hair and watch her eyes soften as she looked up at him. She never looked as though she regarded him as half a man.

She made him feel whole, even though he knew he wasn't.

He felt her stir and with a whoosh, he was engulfed in darkness as the coverlet rained down on him.

He couldn't breathe.

In the back of his mind, he knew it was only cotton and thread, but all he could feel was metal pressing down on him, cutting through his flesh.

He screamed silently, gasping for breath as his fingers clawed at the sheets. His leg kicked, but the limb did nothing to lift the heavy coverlet from his body. Finally, he managed to pull the covers from his face and push them to his waist. Sweat covered every inch of him.

He hadn't had a nightmare that real since just after the accident.

A soft voice broke through the darkness.

"Peter?"

"Go back to sleep, Bet. It was just a bad dream."

"I heard you screaming." Maybe he wasn't silent. He felt her fingers move along his back. "You are drenched."

"I said it was just a dream. I'll sit in the chair, so I don't disturb you." He attempted to roll over, but his limb was caught in the sheets. Giving it several tugs, he could feel the bed clothes wrap tighter, cutting off his circulation. He growled in the darkness.

"Peter, what is it?" Exhaling loudly, he waved his arms against the invisible demons attacking him in the darkness. "Peter." Elizabet's fingers brushed his arm. "Peter!" she pleaded. "Stop it. You are scaring me."

He heard her shuffle down the bed and move around to the side table where she fumbled with the matchbox. With a quick hiss a small light cast a glow to the room and Elizabet lit the lamp on the table. Replacing the globe on the lamp, she shook out the match and the smell of sulfur lingered in the air.

Her eyes were wide as she looked at him. Her hair, which was braided before she went to bed, was starting to come undone from tossing and turning. He reached out and fingered one of the strands that came loose.

"I didn't mean to scare you, Bet."

"What was your dream about?"

"Nothing," he lied. "It was nothing."

"Hmmm. It didn't sound like nothing." She tugged on the sheet. "Lift your leg, I'll get this unwrapped." It took several tugs for his limb to come free of the sheets, and Elizabet tossed them aside. "I guess I'll wash these tomorrow; they are a little drenched."

"I couldn't get comfortable. It's too hot."

"Cooking on an open fire doesn't help."

"I'd like to get you a stove. I saw these cast iron stoves in the catalog."

"We don't need a stove right now, Peter. There are many other things we need before we get a stove." She rolled back on her heels. "Let me get a wet cloth."

"No," his hand snaked out and wrapped around her wrist. "Don't leave me."

"I'm not going anywhere. I'm just going to get the water bowl."

"No. I just need you here with me. Don't leave me."

"I won't leave you."

"Promise?" He leaned up and brushed his lips against hers.

"I promise," she whispered against his lips. "I won't ever leave you."

He pulled her towards him, leaning back down on the bed, praying the words she spoke were true.

CHAPTER NINE

Elizabet scooped eggs onto Peter's plate. "I need to go to town. Would it be alright if I took Boaz?"

"Boaz?" Peter glanced at her before reaching for the toast on the plate in the middle of the table. "I don't recall a Boaz around here."

"I named the horse." She moved around the table and scooped eggs from the pan onto Lukas's plate before placing the rest on her own.

She could hear Lukas chuckle in the background. "I didn't think you named your animals, Peter."

"I don't."

Elizabet smiled as she sat down at the table and took a piece of toast, adding it to her plate. "Shall you say the blessing?" Peter's words were short, and Elizabet echoed with a light amen. "It means *swiftness* in the Bible," she explained around bites of eggs. "I thought it would be a good name for him."

"What do you need to go to town for?"

"This and that."

Peter raised his eyebrow at her. "Any particular this and that?"

"I need to go to the mercantile. And if you must know, I wanted to stop by and see Doc."

Concern flashed across Peter's face. "The doc? Are you ill?"

"No. I just had some questions I needed to ask him." She stole a glance at Lukas. "You know. *Womanly* questions."

Lukas turned bright red and lowered his head, pretending to study his eggs as if they were the most interesting thing he had ever seen.

"I can't make time to take you to town today," Peter said. "Weston was stopping by to talk about moving the cattle for the fall."

"I don't need to be here for that, do I?" Lukas asked.

Peter rolled his shoulders. "Don't think so. You said you might not be here come the fall."

"Might not be here? Why not?" Elizabet demanded.

"Bet. Not now." Elizabet looked at her husband. His hair fell to the side, covering one eye. She longed to reach out and push it aside so she could see him watching her. She could tell there was something on his mind, but he hadn't shared with her, and she didn't want to pry. The words he spoke the other night played over and over in her mind.

"Do you need to take me to town, Peter? Can't I go myself? I shouldn't be too long."

"I don't want you going by yourself. A woman riding alone can get in a heap of trouble."

"Doesn't Mrs. Chapman ride by herself?"

"Marmee?" Lukas asked. "She always carries a pistol with her, and she isn't afraid to use it. Do you know how to shoot, Elizabet?"

"Lukas, let me deal with my wife, please."

"How about I take her into town? I need to go see the blacksmith anyway. We can be back before it's time to feed the horses."

Peter shifted in his chair, his fingers tapping on the table.

"Peter? Please?"

The corners of his mouth turned downward, and his shoulders drooped. With a sigh he pushed his plate of uneaten eggs away from him. "Do what you want,

Elizabet."

Lifting himself from his chair he reached for his crutches, shoving them under his armpits with such a force that Elizabet was surprised he was still standing. He made his way to the porch and pushed the door open with one crutch before hobbling outside.

Elizabet blinked rapidly, her eyes burning as she felt the sting of Peter's rejection. She wasn't sure what she had done to make him angry.

"It isn't you," Lukas said, pulling Peter's plate over and shoveling his uneaten eggs onto his own plate.

"Excuse me?"

"He's mad at himself."

Elizabet swiped her cheek. "I don't know why. He's not done anything to be angry about. And further, I don't think I should be discussing my marriage with you."

"Did Peter ever tell you why I left?"

"He said you left after your Ma died."

"That's true." He shoveled a forkful of eggs into his mouth and chewed thoughtfully. "I actually left because Peter was engaged to be married."

"Engaged?" Bitterness rose in the back of her throat, drowning all taste of her breakfast. Peter never mentioned he was engaged before. She glanced down at the gold ring on her finger. Did this ring belong to someone else? She fingered the ring, feeling the band circling her knuckle.

"Name was Lolly, or something like that. I forget. Pretty little thing." He gave Elizabet a quick wink. "Not as pretty as you, though. Wasn't as good of a cook either."

"Th-thank you, I think."

"I was in the barn with the horses and Lolly stopped by. I thought she came by to visit Peter. Turns out she had something else on her mind."

"You?"

Lukas nodded. "She was my brother's woman." He left the rest unsaid. "Peter came to the barn and Lolly made it appear as though I was trying to seduce her."

Elizabet let out a gasp. "But you weren't."

He shook his head. "Peter's my brother. I'd never betray him. I left the following day."

"What happened to Lolly?"

"She showed up around a week later in the same town I was in. Said she wanted me to marry her."

"Did you?"

Lukas finished the eggs. "Nope. Last I heard she

was working for an establishment that you don't talk about in front of proper ladies."

"But why didn't you come home sooner?"

Shrugging his shoulders, he finished his coffee. "I figured I wanted to see a bit of the West. Time wasn't right."

"Is it true what Peter said? That you are planning on leaving?"

"If I can find me a wife that loves me as much as you love my thick-headed brother, then I'll consider staying. Otherwise, I'm only passing through. I want to be somewhere warmer before the snow falls."

"Love him?" She barely whispered the words. It had only been a week, and she knew she cared for Peter a great deal. Was it possible to fall in love with someone in such a short period of time?

"It's as plain as the nose on your face." Pushing back from the table, he stood and put on his hat. "Truth is, he loves you. He just doesn't want to admit it. Thanks for breakfast. I gotta go fix the loose rail in the paddock and then I'm headed to town. We need some nails and I do have to see the blacksmith. You are more than welcome to come along."

"I'll talk to Peter. Thank you, Lukas."

He strode out the door and she heard Peter's low

voice say something before Lukas's heavy footsteps disappeared towards the barn. Elizabet did the dishes and refilled Peter's coffee cup before walking out to see him.

He was sitting on the chair rocking back and forth with his good leg. His eyes scanned the landscape and Elizabet looked to see what he was staring at. She could see the line of trees near the river and the thicket of briars where she found the blackberry bushes. She wondered if the birds had taken all the fruits. Lukas appeared from the barn with a board on his shoulder and a bucket. She recalled what he said and turned her attention back to her husband.

"I brought you some coffee. I cleaned up, but there is still some toast. I can make you an egg sandwich if you are hungry."

Peter took the cup. "Thank you. I'm not."

Elizabet sat down in the chair next to him. "Peter, what's on your mind."

He turned slowly and looked at her. His eyes which sparkled the day after their wedding were dull. "I'm afraid I won't be able to give you what you deserve."

She picked up his hand and wove her fingers through his. "What do you think I deserve?"

He sipped his coffee thoughtfully. "Maybe your brother was right."

"I'm not following."

"You deserve a man that can take care of you."

"We've had this discussion."

"How about someone that can chase you around the house and swing you about when they catch you?"

"Well. I suppose if I took your crutches, you'd have to put your wooden leg on. You could chase me then." A trace of a smile brushed his lips and Elizabet couldn't help but lift her hand to caress his cheek. "I saw that. What else?"

"I don't want you to feel stuck with an invalid."

"Peter Arkin, I want you to stop that right this instant. You are not an invalid. You are more of a man than most men out there. You need to stop speaking like this. I can't listen to another word, and I must go to town. We forgot several items the last time we were there, and I need to pick up more salve. When do you think you can take me?"

"Weston is stopping by."

"You said that." She exhaled dramatically and dropped her hands in her lap. "I suppose I can give my list to Lukas." She turned her head sharply as Peter mumbled something under his breath. "What was that?"

"At least he'd be able to carry whatever you

needed back from town."

"Peter, what has gotten into you? He's your brother."

"At least he has both of his legs." Peter put his cup on the ground and pushed himself up from the chair. Grasping for his crutches he stumbled towards the railing. Elizabet flew to his side to steady him, her fingers wrapping around his arms to hold him steady.

"I've got you," she said softly. When he stopped rocking, she leaned forward and handed him a crutch. "I'll always have you," she said, handing him the second one. Peter steadied himself and turned to make his way back inside. Picking up his empty cup she called to him. "There is one thing your brother doesn't have. He told me himself."

Peter paused for a moment and straightened himself up to his full height. "What's that?"

"He doesn't have a wife who loves him."

Lukas doesn't have a wife who loves him.

Elizabet's words rang hollow in Peter's ears. Lukas could have any woman he wanted. Why he

could even have Bet; all Lukas needed to do was show her what a complete failure Peter was as a man.

Peter, however, was doing a mighty fine job of doing that himself without anyone's help.

Lukas had already stolen one woman; he didn't want to think about his brother stealing another. Yet, the idea had already been planted and was taking root through his every thought. It tormented his every moment, and even those while he was asleep.

He must be going mad.

He could never let Bet know.

Lukas doesn't have a wife who loves him.

The urge to hit something was strong, but he wasn't a man of violence.

Peter had never hit a man before. He was a man of words.

Peter didn't hit Lukas when he caught his brother with Lolly in the barn.

He didn't hit Weston when his friend tried to take the whiskey bottle from him.

He didn't hit Elizabet's brother when Todd pushed her to the ground. The last one was the hardest of all.

Instead, he managed to solve each of those situations with words, no matter how tempting it would be to pummel someone into the ground.

But now, the urge to pound someone, something, anything… rose up inside him and burned with an anger so volatile it would consume everything around him.

He needed to get away.

But where would he run to?

Ha! That was rich. He had one good leg.

He wasn't running anywhere.

He might as well take Elizabet to town. He could get away from the farm and perhaps he would have calmed down by the time they returned. She had a way of soothing him unlike anyone else.

As he turned, Peter spied her Momma's Bible sitting on her rocking chair. The thick spine was worn from use and the front cover was cracked and faded. He hopped over and reached down, running his finger along the embossed words on the front.

I want to teach our children to read from the Bible.

Lukas doesn't have a wife who loves him.

Suddenly Elizabet's meaning became clear.

Did Elizabet really love him?

Or was Lukas just saying that?

Spinning on his crutch, he hobbled to the porch and prayed that Elizabet hadn't gone off into the yard. She wasn't on the porch, but his coffee cup was sitting on the railing. His eyes darted around to find her standing near the paddock with Lukas.

Looking at her took his breath away. She ran her fingers through her blonde hair, and it slid across her shoulder before cascading down her back. Peter knew how soft those strands were when they slipped through his own fingers.

She turned her head slightly to listen to something Lukas said, and Peter could see where the sun had kissed her cheeks. She was dressed in the new frock from the mercantile. It fit her perfectly – the bright blue fabric clinging to every curve, before flaring out from her waist.

She leaned forward to say something to Lukas and waved her hand slightly in the air. Lukas let forth a laugh that hardened Peter's stomach. Stepping from the porch, he swung his crutches and moved his leg towards the paddock.

"Bet!" His fists clenched around the handles of his crutches, the wood digging into his fingers and palms. She didn't hear him. He saw her hand move once more… *then it happened.*

As if time was moving slowly, Peter watched as Lukas's hand lifted and skimmed across her blonde tresses. Elizabet lifted her hand and pushed Lukas's arm away and screamed.

Without shifting his grip, Peter stumbled forward, struggling to reach his wife as quickly as possible. Moments later he'd cleared the yard with the speed of a man on two legs and a blinding rage that would only be quelled when Lukas was on the ground.

Pushing his way between Lukas and Elizabet, Peter lifted the crutch nearest his full leg so he wouldn't fall, and pointed it at Lukas's chest.

"Take your hands off my wife," he snarled pushing Lukas back into the wooden rail of the paddock.

"Hey, now," Lukas said. "I was only trying to…"

"I saw what you were trying to do. If you ever touch her again, I will tear your arm…"

"Peter!" Elizabet cried, placing her hand on his arm, and lowering the crutch. "It was a bug."

"I don't care." Words weren't registering. Air rushed from his lungs as he tried to speak. "Get your basket, Bet. I'm taking you to town."

"What about Mr. Chapman?"

Peter never took his eyes from his brother, his lip curling in disgust at Lukas standing there.

Lukas met the challenge, his arms crossing over his chest, his nostrils flaring like Weston's prized bull, his chin jutting forward in defiance.

"Lukas can stay here to meet him," Peter snarled.

"Peter..."

"Now, Elizabet." His tone had his wife scurrying to gather her few items. He watched as Lukas peered over Peter's shoulder to follow Elizabet racing back to the house.

"If you aren't careful, brother..."

Lukas didn't have a chance to finish his thought as Peter dropped his crutch and let his fist connect with Lukas's jaw. His knuckles crunched as his tightened hand met flesh and bone; and he gasped as pain radiated up his arm causing him to stumble backwards.

Losing his grip on the crutch he held, Peter staggered, and he tried to keep his balance with his one good leg, but his efforts were futile. With his empty hand he circled the air, trying to find something to stop his fall. Just as his crutch slipped in the dirt, he felt a sharp jerk on the front of his shirt.

Snapping his eyes forward, he opened them wide as Lukas grinned, blood and spittle oozing from his lips.

"You think you know what you are talking about," Lukas spit blood on the ground. "You didn't know then. You don't know now."

"I know you seduced Lolly. I'm not going to have you do the same to my wife."

Lukas released Peter's shirt. As Peter staggered backwards, Lucas grabbed him once more. "I never did a thing to Lolly. I left because I knew it was going to cause more trouble than she was worth."

Peter's head started to hurt. "She told me you sent for her and that is why she was leaving."

Lukas's face twisted in confusion. "I never did. I don't know how she found me. Once she did, I left that town. Then the next. Then the one after that." He pushed Peter towards the paddock fencing so he could keep his balance and then handed him the crutch that fell on the ground. "I swear brother, I never did anything. I would never hurt you, or Elizabet." His eyes flickered to the house. "She's coming back."

"Why were you touching her?"

"She had a June bug caught in her hair. That's all."

Lukas dragged his hand down his face and for once Peter could see how ragged his brother looked. Eyes that twinkled looked tired at the corners. His skin was dull, and he just looked ... *sad.*

"I-I," Peter stammered. He felt ashamed. It would serve him right if Lukas punched him back.

"You know she loves you."

Peter looked out at the fields. He was too ashamed to look at his brother.

"Don't be a fool, Peter. You are going to push her away if you aren't careful. Any man would be right lucky to have a woman like Elizabet for a wife. Make sure you deserve her as much as she loves you."

Peter glanced back to see Elizabet scampering past them towards the barn. Underneath her arm he noticed she was carrying his wooden leg. Looking back at Lukas he nodded. "I will. Forgive me?"

Lukas nodded and pulled Peter into his strong embrace, slapping him on the back. "That's what brothers are for. Get your wife to town and I'll follow, after I meet with Mr. Chapman."

Peter nodded and hobbled towards the barn, his pride still stinging like the pain in his knuckles.

CHAPTER TEN

Elizabet rode in silence next to her husband until she couldn't take it anymore.

"Are you going to tell me what happened back there?"

"No."

"Is Lukas going to be at the house when we get home?"

Peter looked at her and shrugged. "I don't know."

"At least I have his list."

"Why would you have his list?"

"I told him I was going to the mercantile and he had to go to the blacksmith."

"Hmmm."

She reached over and touched Peter's skinned

knuckles. "You hit him, didn't you?"

"Bet, that's between Lukas and me."

"The same way whatever you said to my brother was between you and him?"

"Yep."

She leaned over the bench and pulled her basket over the seat. Pulling out the small glass jar, she returned the basket, then grabbed Peter's hand and placed it on her knee.

"You and your brother are very stubborn." Opening the jar, she rubbed her finger inside to scrape the remaining salve from the bottom of the glass. "Stubborn brothers have a tendency to upset everyone."

Slathering the ointment on his knuckles, she closed the jar and tossed it back in the basket before rubbing each finger, coating his torn skin with the protective jelly.

"Are you upset?"

"Well, I'm not pleased. I don't want to see you or your brother fighting."

"We aren't fighting anymore."

Elizabet smiled. "That's good. I like your brother."

"That's what I'm afraid of."

"He is very much like you. Strong. Honorable.

Kind."

"He told me he was getting a bug out of your hair."

"He was. There was a June... Peter Arkin." Realization dawned on her. "Were you jealous?"

Peter looked forward at the horse pulling the buckboard. "I might have been," he said softly.

"Whatever for? I'm married to you, Peter. You." She threaded her hand through his elbow and rested it on his arm. "I think our vows said in sickness and in health. In grace and stubbornness."

Peter let out a loud laugh. "I must have been in pain. I don't recall those last ones."

"Lukas told me about Lolly." The smile disappeared from Peter's face. "She was a fool to treat you that way. I want you to know that as much as I like your brother, it will only be as that. A brother. You are my husband. The only man I will ever love."

"So, you love me?" The hint of a smile played across his lips.

"I think I do." She bounced her fingers on his arm. "I know we've not been married very long, but just in the time we've been together I have come to care for you a great deal."

Peter curled his fingers around her hand. "I feel the same."

"Is that your way of saying you love me?"

"Yes," he smiled. "Yes, it is."

"I hope Lukas stays."

"Why's that?"

"He's your brother, and family is important."

"I recall you saying that you wanted your own home."

She leaned her head on his shoulder. "I have my own home. I don't think that Lukas would ask me to leave."

"Perhaps we need to find him a wife."

"Maybe. He said that perhaps he should find one this morning at breakfast."

"He did? I don't recall that."

"You were on the porch. It might be good for him to settle down and not drift from town to town anymore."

"Weston was saying that Marmee thinks of herself as quite the matchmaker now."

"Well, then maybe she can find someone for Lukas."

The rest of the trip they conspired on the type of wife they imagined Lukas needed. They were laughing so hard, that they could scarcely draw breath when they pulled next to the mercantile.

"Want to give me your list?" Peter asked, as he set the brake against the wheel.

"Why don't you come with me? I need to see Doc."

His brows furrowed with concern. "Are you ill?"

"No." Jumping down from the wagon she reached behind the bench and picked up his wooden leg. "I wanted to see if we could find a leg that fit you better. Or we'll find some leather and padding, and I'll fashion something for the top."

Peter looked at her for a moment and she swore there were tears glistening in his eyes. Finally, he nodded and lowered himself from the seat. Balancing on his crutches, he followed her across the narrow street to the wooden building that boasted Dr. Mueller's practice. Elizabet held the door open while Peter hobbled in.

"Hello!" Elizabet called.

Peter sat in one of the chairs in the foyer. Soon a man of approximately fifty years appeared from behind a large curtain. His hair was blonde and falling over on one side. He wore square spectacles held to his ears by thin wires with blue eyes that appeared larger than normal from behind the thick lenses. He wasn't tall, but he wasn't short, and he had the appearance of someone who enjoyed a good meal every now and then.

Doc, as he was known, was one of the first settlers of Flat River and knew every resident in town.

"Peter! What brings you to town today? And Elizabet. I hope nothing is wrong."

"My wife wanted to stop by and see you."

"I was wondering if you might help me make Peter's leg more comfortable for him," Elizabet said, holding up Peter's prosthetic.

"I can do something better than that. Come on back." Doc pulled the curtain aside and ushered Elizabet and Peter into a small examination area. "This came on the stage yesterday. I was going to stop by and see you, but you saved me the trip." He pulled a box from the side of his desk. "I've not even had a chance to open it."

"What is it?" Peter asked. The box was at least three feet long.

Doc stood the box up on its end and taking a knife from his desk, he slid it down the side of the packaging. "Watch out." The box opened and a contraption unlike anything Elizabet had ever seen fell out on the floor. "I sent away for it over six months ago. It finally arrived. Can you believe it?" Doc lifted the item and stood it up.

It looked like a flesh-colored foot that gave way to a wooden leg, then to a leather encasement and it was surrounded by brass fittings.

"What is it?" she asked.

Doc spun it around so Elizabet and Peter could see it from all sides. "It's called an A. A. Marks Artificial Limb. Notice how it looks more like a natural leg. There is an ankle-joint that will allow you to walk without the stiffness associated with the long gait of your current leg. The entire upper portion of your leg will be encased so you don't have the pressure of your stump against the wood. And here, beneath where your knee is, it actually bends for you."

"What's the foot made from?" Elizabet asked, looking at the lifelike toes.

"Rubber. Layers of Rubber."

"I can't wear a leg like that. The rubber would tear right up."

"There is wood inside the rubber, so it minimizes wearing. But you can actually slide this into a boot."

"So, it won't look like he is wearing a false leg at all?" Elizabet put her finger up to her mouth. Peter was looking at the contraption with awe. "What do you think?" she asked.

"I've never seen anything like it in my life."

"Of course not," Doc guffawed. "They haven't made many of these yet and I was able to get you one of the first."

"I don't know if I can afford it."

"I wrote to the company. Asked for a medical sample. I'll write an article about it after six months." His eyes twinkled. "Shall we try it on you?"

"Will it fit?" Peter was doubtful.

"It should be close. I sent them everything I knew about you."

"I'll step outside for a moment." Elizabet went back to the waiting area, and she could hear Doc and Peter wrestle with the artificial limb. She tried not to giggle as she heard sounds of excitement and then frustration come from behind the curtain. Finally, Peter called her to come see.

Elizabet peeked behind the curtain and gasped as she saw her husband standing tall. He was much taller than when he wore the wooden boot she carried. His shoulders were back, and he stood proud, as he waited for her reaction. She wouldn't have been able to tell he was missing a limb, apart from the slight bulge in the knee area from the joint mechanism, and the pink rubber toes peeking out from his black wool pants.

"Oh Peter!" She blinked rapidly, as tears started to burn. "You look…" words escaped her.

"Handsome?" he offered.

She laughed. "Tall." She moved forward and gave him a hug. Peter's arms wrapped around her, and he kissed the top of her hair. "Handsome, too," she conceded. "How does it feel?"

"Like a glove."

Doc took off his glasses and wiped them on the hem of his shirt. "I want you to take it and use it for a week, then come back and we'll see if we need to make any adjustments."

"We'll have to get you a pair of boots from the mercantile," Elizabet said.

"That's a purchase I'm happy to make."

Doc offered Peter a pair of socks. Peter slid it on to protect the rubber foot and headed towards the door, but not before Elizabet gave Doc a hug.

"You go ahead, Peter. I have a quick question for the doctor."

"You sure you need me to go?"

"It's a rather delicate question."

Peter looked at her for a moment and then his eyebrows went up. "I'll take these to the wagon and meet you there."

She watched Peter leave the doctor's office and waited for the sound of the door to close.

"What can I help you with, Mrs. Arkin?" Doc asked.

"I have questions about babies."

One year later

Elizabet opened her eyes slightly and promptly shut them again.

She needed to get curtains made to cover the windows.

Stretching her arms above her head, she rolled over and reached her hands, grabbing at air, instead of the solid muscles of her husband's back. Keeping her eyes closed, she patted the bed, feeling the plump mattress and the sheets which Peter had pulled back in place.

Opening one eye, she groaned again as a twinge in her back insisted that it was time to awaken.

What time was it? And where was Peter?

Rolling over once more, she swung her feet to the floor and felt for her day shoes with her toes, sliding her feet into the soft leather.

"Good morning, little ones," she cooed, opening

her eyes, and rubbing her belly. "We'll take care of morning things first, and then we'll go find Poppa. How does that sound?" Another twinge in Elizabet's back gave no mercy to her delicate bladder. "Alright, alright, I'm getting up."

She couldn't believe it when the doctor told her that she was carrying two precious lives.

"There must be something in the water," Marmee had laughed. She should know; there were at least three sets of twins in the Chapman family.

Grabbing her wrapper, Elizabet placed it around her shoulders and disappeared behind a screen to take care of her morning ablutions before getting dressed and going in search of her husband.

"Peter?" She pulled closed the bedroom door behind her and entered the great room.

With the growing family, they decided it made sense to add several rooms, so Elizabet and Peter weren't sleeping on the floor near the fireplace.

They expanded the house and added two bedrooms to the main floor, plus a larger pantry and a separate kitchen area. The upstairs became Lukas' private quarters, but he spent most of his time outside with the cowboys, only returning home when the weather became unbearable.

It took three months to build the addition, with

Peter and Lukas working on it between the other chores around the farm. The last room was finished as the first snowflakes started to fall.

Peter had his own surprise for Elizabet. A large cast iron stove with four burners, a wood box and an oven arrived at the mercantile just for her. It took four horses to carry it out to the farm and three men to unload it. Elizabet couldn't stop peppering her husband's face with kisses as they uncrated the beautiful black cooker.

"Came all the way from New York," he told her. He had ordered from a catalog at the mercantile.

She was thrilled that they had an actual bedroom to sleep in, with a bed that wasn't on the floor. Peter was quite the furniture maker, and Elizabet thought he might have found a new occupation that could fill his mind and his hands.

She called her husband once more but didn't hear him. Moving to the kitchen table to see if he left a note, there wasn't anything but a plate of fresh biscuits on the table with a small jar of strawberry jam she made earlier in the week.

Taking one of the biscuits, she smeared it with jam and carried it outside in search of her husband. The summer sun was already high in the sky, signaling it must be close to noon. She couldn't believe that she slept half the day away. What must her husband think of her?

Her conscience twinged as she recalled how harshly she judged Lucinda for being tired all the time.

Popping the last bit of biscuit in her mouth, she chewed as she looked around the yard for any sign of her husband or brother-in-law. The buckboard was missing, which meant either Lukas went to town or Peter did. She doubted Peter would leave without telling her.

She strained her ears to listen for any sound near the house, but only the sound of the chickens scratching in the dirt met her ears. She brushed the crumbs from her fingers and headed towards the barn.

The sound of Peter's rich voice singing echoed through the barn as she opened the door. She could see him in the corner, sitting on a bench with a piece of wood locked between his knees. His hands moved back and forth, carving an intricate pattern along one edge of the wood with a metal chisel.

She silently moved into the barn and stood in the shadow so she could watch her husband. The muscles under his shirt flexed with each turn of the chisel. His new leg was bent perfectly to hold the piece of wood in place, and he wasn't grimacing as he did with his former prosthetic. It didn't rub his skin raw as often as his former appendage, but Elizabet still spent every night tending to her husband's delicate skin before bed.

Rose Arden jested that the mercantile couldn't keep in Vaseline's Wonder Jelly since Elizabet started telling everyone about it.

"What are you working on?" Bet asked.

"The second cradle." He smiled as he put the chisel down and extended his arm. "I'm glad you are finally awake," he said huskily. "Come here, Bet."

Elizabet felt his timbre all the way down to her toes, which were curling in her boots. Walking in between his legs, he placed both his hands on her swollen belly and planted a kiss against the rough fabric of her day dress. Her fingers crept through his dark hair and gently pulled at it.

"I'll need to cut your hair again. It's getting long. I've been negligent, husband."

"Never." He kissed her belly again. "You've needed your rest. Marmee said she was extremely tired when carrying her twins."

"Thank you for making biscuits. Or did Lukas make them this morning?"

"Addie brought them by. She and Lukas went on a picnic at the church today."

"Addie?"

Peter's hands moved up to her neck and he planted kisses along her chin.

"He met her at Marmee's. I guess she is a niece or cousin or something. But you didn't come out here to ask about that."

His lips captured hers and Elizabet closed her eyes, leaning in to be closer. Peter's hand gently caressed her belly in a protective gesture as shivers raced across her skin. She felt herself swoon as he deepened the kiss.

How could this man affect her this way?

Peter must have felt her sway, as his arms wrapped around her, quickly holding her in place. He pulled her down on his lap and she felt the metal of the braces attaching the prosthesis to his upper leg cutting into her skin.

"I don't want to hurt you."

"You won't. Just let me hold you for a second. Every time I hold you, you make me feel whole. I love you so much, Bet."

Elizabet turned slightly. "I love... Oh, Peter!" She pushed away from him and started walking back towards the barn door. The urge to retch was overpowering. Blackness consumed her vision, and stars appeared behind her eyes. She reached her hand out, struggling against the blindness to find the barn door for support. Her lungs compressed in her chest as she tried to gasp, but filling her lungs was futile. In seconds, the pain released, and she could breathe again.

Peter was at her side immediately. "Bet? What is it?" She reached her arm behind her trying to find him, her arm flailing wildly. She finally grasped his hand; she could feel him shaking. "Bet?"

Inhaling deeply, she pressed her hand to her lower back. "I just had this horrible pain go across my entire back and down my legs."

"Is it the babies?"

"I don't know. I've had these tremors all night, but now they are taking my breath away."

"We need to get you to the house." Peter turned her around and leaned down, sweeping Elizabet into his arms.

Elizabet wrapped her arms around his neck and tried not to lean into his chest. She felt Peter pull her closer.

"Peter, put me down, I can walk."

"Hush, wife. I can carry you."

Warmth radiated through her, and she closed her

eyes, listening to the soft sound of brass rubbing against wood. He would never have had the confidence to carry her before now.

In fact, his confidence had returned ten-fold since Doc Mueller fitted him properly for the new leg.

She concentrated on the sound of the door opening and closing. She listened to the sound of his boots thud against the floor towards their bedroom. Soon the warmth of Peter's embrace was gone as he gently placed her on the bed.

He kissed her forehead. "I need to go get the doc."

Elizabet nodded. It was becoming too painful to breathe again. When she could finally take a breath, she waved to Peter. "I know. Go. You would probably be better going to the Chapman's first. They can send someone for Doc."

"Don't go anywhere." He kissed her forehead once more.

"Well, I was thinking of taking Boaz and riding to town, but I'll wait for a bit," she teased.

"I'll make sure to take him with me." With one last glance, he was gone.

Elizabet laid back on the pillows and closed her eyes, a single tear rolling down her cheek as she waited for her husband to return. She must have dozed off as she was stirred by the sound of movement in the main room.

"Peter?" she called. She was so parched; her voice came out as a weak cry. When she didn't get a response, she called once more.

A shadow filled the room. "No, It's me, Luk… Elizabet!" Lukas ran to her side. "Where's Peter?"

Elizabet grabbed Lukas's hand. "He went to get the doctor. The babies are coming."

"It's too soon. Addie!" he called. A young woman, just a bit older than Elizabet came to the room. "What do you know about birthing babies?"

"May I come in?" a soft voice asked. Elizabet nodded. She just wanted the pain to end. She felt a small hand on her belly and the soft voice counted out loud. "Those babies are coming now. You go and boil some water and find me some linen sheets. I'll also need a bowl of clean, cold water."

"Linens are in the cupboard over there." Elizabet pointed to the corner.

"Out. Out." The woman named Addie shooed Lukas out of the room. "Once you get the water boiling, I want you to ride and go get Marmee." He nodded and gave Elizabet's hand a squeeze before disappearing from the room.

"Who are you?" Elizabet asked, looking at the woman walking over to the bed. She was very pretty with long brown hair pulled back with a black ribbon.

The mattress dipped when the woman sat down. "My name is Addison Aland. I was visiting Aunt Ingrid and Uncle Weston for the summer. You're Elizabeth?"

"Bet… Elizabet."

"Lukas told me all about you. How long have you been having pain?"

"All night, but nothing like this."

"Well babies come on their own time, so save your strength."

Elizabet closed her eyes and listened to Addie's soothing voice. Soon she was helping Elizabet sit up in the bed and push her babies into the world. The strong, angry cries of healthy newborns filled the air and Elizabet fell back against the pillows with a sob.

"You have two beautiful daughters," Addie said, handing a baby to Elizabet.

There was a knock on the door and Marmee Chapman came in.

"It looks like you have everything under control here. Excellent work, Addison. How are you feeling, Elizabet?" She placed a cool hand against Elizabet's forehead.

"Where's Peter?"

"He's outside with the rest of the men. I sent one of my men to town for the doctor, but it looks like you did just fine. Addie, you finish cleaning up the babies, I'll tend to Elizabet and then Peter can come in and see his children."

Addie stayed and made dinner, much to Lukas's delight. When everyone finally left, and the babies were settled into a bassinet, Peter joined his wife in bed. His back rested against the wall, with his arm wrapped around his wife. Elizabet rested her head on his shoulder as they talked softly about their beautiful children and how thankful they were for the neighbors who helped them. Her eyes were growing heavy as Peter traced circles on her arm.

"You aren't disappointed they aren't sons?" Elizabet asked, pulling the coverlet up to her shoulders.

Peter kissed the top of her head. "Never. I can't think of anything that makes me happier than two little girls that look just like their mother."

"I thought you wanted sons, though."

Peter continued to trace circles. "I think any man does." He gave a light chuckle. "It just means we will have to keep having children, Bet."

"You are incorrigible, Peter," she giggled, "but I love you. Have you thought about names?"

"I was thinking we could name one after our mothers."

"Rose, after your mother. Beulah after mine?"

"I think that has a nice ring. Rose Beulah Arkin. What do you think?"

"Hmmm," Elizabet replied sleepily. "It is beautiful. What about our second daughter?"

"How about Ingrid Elizabet?"

"Ingrid?" She snuggled into her husband's arms and allowed his warmth to envelop her. "Where did that name come from?"

"That's Marmee's real name. After all, she brought us together."

"Rose and Ingrid. Those names are perfect."

My family is whole, she thought, as she drifted off to sleep.

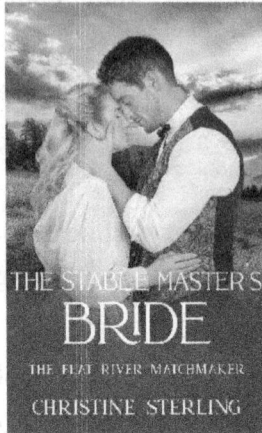

be strictly a business arrangement.

Can Hiram fight his growing attraction to Hannah? When tragedy strikes can Hannah find the courage to fight for her new family? What happens when Hiram starts to fall in love with his new wife – is it enough to make a marriage of convenience very real?

COMING JANUARY 2023

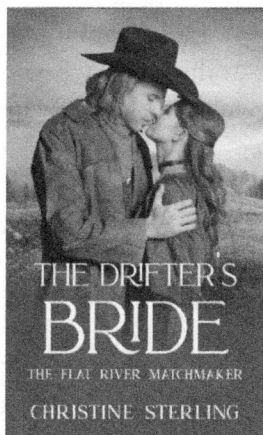

A woman escaping society's expectations of marriage; a man with nothing to offer, a match that threatens to tear two families apart.

Addison Aland came west to escape the pressure of an arranged marriage. Her family is convinced that once she experiences dirty cowboys, cow patties and the lack of retail establishments she will hightail it back home to be a high-society wife. What she didn't count on was Lukas Arkin making her question everything she thought she knew about life and love.

Lukas Arkin has been drifting from town to town for nearly ten years. Tired of wandering he finally returns home to Flat River to find his brother married with a family on the way. When he hires the local matchmaker to help him find a wife, he realizes the one woman he wants is the one he can't have.

What happens when Lukas falls for Addison? Will he be able to let Addison go when he finds out that Marmee had matched him to another? *Can he convince Marmee that Addison should be The Drifter's Bride?*

The Drifter's Bride – Coming January 2023.

To find out more about this series, its characters, and all the series set in this lovely fictional town, visit www.flatrivernebraska.com.

ABOUT CHRISTINE STERLING

USA Today bestselling author **CHRISTINE STERLING** writes small-town inspirational romances with a touch of humor. Most of her stories take place in the plains of Nebraska or Colorado, but she will write wherever there are cowboys needing to find love. Her favorite stories involve tight-knit families, and you will often find that her characters cross over in many of her stories.

She lives on a farm in Pennsylvania with her husband, four dogs, and one spoiled cat, aka The Floof. She can often be found in her garden with a notebook and a cup of tea.

Made in the USA
Monee, IL
27 April 2025

16438642R00090